THE RUBY COLLECTION

The Society of Women Writers WA

ISBN-13: 978-1-922727-00-8

Linellen Press
265 Boomerang Road
Oldbury, Western Australia
www.linellenpress.com.au

Dedication

To Ruth Reid, our much-loved Patron.
To all the members who have supported The Society by rejoining year after year, and especially to Molly Smith for being the first member to reach forty years of continuous membership.

Contents

Acknowledgments

Producing a quality publication is a team effort. I, therefore, thank the selection panel of Jan Altmann, Lucy Cotton, Sue Colyer and Helen Iles for reading and selecting the contributions that achieved publication and ensuring the theme challenge of mentioning the word 'Ruby' was maintained throughout, to Maria Bonar for proofreading the final draft, and to Linellen Press for undertaking the book and cover design of this, our 40th-anniversary anthology.

Helen Iles

Chairperson

The Society of Women Writer WA

The Lost Ring

My mother was a practical no-frills type of woman. She dressed in a simple, home-made sort of way that was always a little behind the times. When we went to town shopping, the other ladies were so much smarter in their colourful dresses, hats and gloves, much less home-made. As could be expected, my mother was not much interested in jewelry. I had only ever seen her wearing her simple, gold wedding band. When I asked to have my ears pierced so that I could wear earrings, she told me firmly that it was not natural to have holes in one's ears! Make-up was out of the question.

Shortly after she passed away, my father presented me with a small cloth bag which contained her jewelry. I was surprised that she had owned any jewelry but delighted to receive it. There were red and green glass neckpieces and some old-style brooches, but the piece that attracted my attention was an elegant little gold ring set with a row of small ruby and diamond chips. My father explained that this had been my mother's engagement ring. On looking closely, I could see that one of the ruby chips was missing. Perhaps this was why she didn't wear it. Perhaps she couldn't find a jeweler to repair it, or perhaps she was just not interested. I put it away in a small, silver box with a few other pieces of jewelry. I then forgot about it, and also didn't wear it.

Soon after I married, I looked again at this little ruby and diamond ring and decided that I would have it repaired so I could wear it with my own engagement ring. This involved replacing the ruby chip and a complete remodeling of the ring so that the settings could be made more secure.

I enjoyed wearing this small ring but tended to keep it for special occasions. At all other times it remained in its small, silver box on my dressing table.

One evening after dressing for such an occasion I removed the lid of this box to take out the ring and put it on my finger. To my dismay, it was not there. I stood holding the lid and peering into the box for some time. Then I carefully tipped all the other rings, earrings, and trinkets out onto the bed thinking that my ruby ring had simply worked its way to the bottom and been covered over. Perplexed but not concerned I replaced these contents thinking that somehow I must have carelessly placed the ring somewhere else.

Over time I searched everywhere, even the inside pockets of my handbags, in case I had removed the ring during some function and dropped it into one of these pockets. Strangely, I could not recall the last time I had worn it. Still more confused than distressed, I concluded that the disappearance of my ruby ring was 'just one of those things', and that it probably would never be found.

Then the dreams started. In the first dream I found myself on a misty, green country lane. I was walking along towards the sound of running, splashing water. Suddenly the mist drew back on either side, like curtains when we rise to greet a new day. Soft sunlight revealed a colourful, flowery vision that rose and spread to meet me. It spilled down the banks towards a stream of clear, sparkling water. Just as this delightful dream began to fade, I caught sight of a female figure standing on the opposite bank. So pleasant and peaceful was this dream that it stayed with me long afterwards. I had not realised before that we do indeed dream in colour. The whites, reds, yellows and pinks of these flowers were so vibrant that I can still see them to this day.

Recurring dreams, we are told, indicate psychological problems that need to be dealt with, usually unresolved situations or difficult relationships. My flower dream did not suggest any such difficulties, but it did return. It was not so much recurring as continuing. When the next one came, I was back amongst the flowers and right on the edge of the stream. Suddenly, the female figure which had so quickly faded away on the previous occasion was again on the opposite bank, but much clearer. This time I saw a young woman, possibly only fifteen or sixteen, walking at a leisurely pace along the bank. As in dreams, the image probably lasted only a few seconds, but I was able to notice that she was wearing a long, russet-coloured dress of coarsely woven fabric, gathered at the waist and the wrists. Over this was a long, white pinafore-style apron. Her long chestnut-coloured hair was held back by a neat, white cap.

Every few steps she stopped and bent down to gather up a few leaves and flowers and carefully place them in an open basket held in her left hand. Just as it seemed that she was turning to look in my direction, the image faded, and I woke up. I felt disturbed but more curious than fearful. The more I thought about it the more I felt that she had tried to tell me something. The story was far from finished.

A few nights later this mysterious figure visited me again. Again, she was walking by the stream and carrying her basket. This time, with her was an older woman who seemed to be showing her which plants to pick and add to her basket. Her dress was the same, and suggested a time long past, probably the seventeenth century. In addition, foraging for plants under the guidance of an older woman indicated that she was learning something about them. Because of the times in which they seemed to be living this probably had something to do with their healing practices.

The final dream was more like a nightmare. Inside a small, stone building, three sombre-looking men in dark-grey coats and steeple-crowned hats sat within a high pulpit-like structure. Two others sat at a long table in front of the pulpit with a pile of papers between them. They all looked towards the doorway as two men half-carried a young, semi-conscious woman with her hands bound through the small courtroom, and although she was barely able to stand, they placed her in front of the sombre men in hats. As she turned to look in my direction, I saw that her face was bruised and swollen.

'What are the charges?' asked one of the dark-suited men in the pulpit.

'That she has practised healing by means of witchcraft,' was the reply. 'She has been seen in the woods and down by the stream gathering so called healing plants with her grandmother, who is known to practise such wickedness.'

When it came time for the young accused to enter a plea, it was explained to her that as this was her first offence, and that using herbs to treat ailments was not in itself a cause for serious punishment, the penalty would not be severe. A guilty verdict, however, would still mean some punishment. She would be sent from her village, never to return. She would be released but would be well advised to give up her irregular practices of using herbal remedies if she did not wish to be forever branded a witch.

After some time, she gathered enough strength and courage to respond. 'If the charge is making herbal cures, then I am guilty,' she declared in a tearful, trembling voice, 'but I was only trying to help people.' At this declaration, several people in the courtroom came forward to testify that they had tried potions made up by this young 'witch', and that they had indeed felt much better for it.

At this, the poor girl fell to her knees tearfully pleading to be forgiven. She promised that if she could stay in the village, she would never gather herbs again. The judge, however, was not convinced. He passed the official sentence that she was to leave the village that very day and never return. Slowly she rose to her feet and turned towards the door. Some of those inside the room tried to comfort her. Outside, a red-faced, angry mob surged forward. Some shouted for her to be thrown into the river. Others brandished knives. They screamed, 'Cut off her hands.'

I panicked. I called out. My own voice woke me. 'Stop, leave her alone'.

She seemed to hear me. In despair, she threw up her hands. She covered her face and disappeared. As she raised her hands, I saw it clearly, my ruby ring.

I will never know what happened to this beautiful young woman, or who she was. What I do know is that next morning I looked in my jewellery box and there, right on top, was my ruby ring. I will never know how this came about, but the ruby is my birth stone, and my mother's. Maybe it was also the birthstone of this courageous young woman who lived, and possibly died horribly, so long ago.

Jan Altmann

What is a Ruby?

Rubies' chemical equation
Unlocks the key
By its revelation
You are family to sapphires.

Scientifically both are varieties of corundum and impurities create the colour. Chromium makes the red in rubies so anything not red is a sapphire. (Pink is a lighter red and that is where the ruby classification starts)

Rich, redolent, red
Unique undying symbol of love
Beautiful union of love and passion
You shimmer with captured passion

The heart quickens and the pulse beats faster; the ruby ring ignites passion in some and greed in others. Emotions engaged. Fingers caress the red stone. Romance cares not for equations. It feels. The stone glints in the sun, creating fire rainbows.

Whether science or romance, you shine your red brightly for all to see.

For me, the ruby contains the fire to spark creativity, the vibrational energy of protection, and carries a frequency to promote health.

Regardless of the story, rubies are magnificent.

Linda Blackshaw

Ashfall

Behind me, something hissed. I gathered my skirts and jumped forward, ducking and diving through the bushes, leaping over fallen branches until I could run no more. Tunnelling under a thicket of brambles, I drew deep gasping breaths. I willed myself to shrink and be still, at any moment expecting claws to grasp my ankles and yank me out into the open.

Nothing happened...

I gradually crawled out of the thicket. The path was clear. What on earth had been following me? Some monster which caught and killed my companions while I bathed in the river? What could have caused such deep claw marks on their bodies and left what remained of their heads in a halo of blood? I relived the horror of stumbling over them and slipping on the gory track where they had fallen. A delicate cone-shaped object with a lustrous ruby stone set in its base lay between them. I picked up the curio and examined it before tucking it in my pocket.

Why had I let them persuade me to travel through the wasteland of Ashfall? As survivors, we had little enough, but we were safe in our own little valley. I was content to have sufficient food and shelter as well as the company of my two friends. If others had survived in similar little patches of sweet country, well, let them trek over the wasteland to find us.

What will become of me now? Shall I return to my valley and risk encountering the unknown beast, or forge ahead in the hope of finding a band of kindred spirits? A cascade of rocks from a nearby hill, followed by a loud hissing caused me to flee north. I ran, sweat coating me and stinging the scratches on my face and arms caused by the brambles. I lost all sense of direction on the winding path. The day was ending and I feared the lonely night. Ahead, the setting sun framed a spectral silhouette. I stopped abruptly, heart pounding. At my back, more hissing. Danger behind me. Danger ahead.

A sudden burst of rage propelled me onward. I wanted to attack my enemy, bludgeon it, gouge its eyes out, kick it, and kill it. I snatched up a stout branch and rushed forward screaming as the shadow loomed, but was suddenly pulled sideways from the path.

A stranger's voice in my ear, "Quickly, up the ladder! It cannot climb."

My hand was thrust onto a rope ladder, barely visible in the dusk. I scrabbled to climb, propelled upwards by the urgent hands of my rescuer, who ascended closely behind me until we tumbled over the rim of the hill to safety.

I looked down at an elaborate contraption cobbled from a dismembered tractor, topped with mismatched cogs and gears, steaming and hissing down the path. Plant-like tendrils sprouted from its roof, while an odd luminescent band of ectoplasm appeared to have attached itself to the windscreen. Like goldfish in a glass bowl, I saw the disembodied faces of my two friends bobbing around inside, their mouths stretched wide in silent screams revealed by the silver light of the moon. I gasped and covered my eyes.

When the tractor reached the base of the hill, my pocket buzzed with heat and vibration. I pulled out the cone-shaped object, my thumb pressing on the now glowing ruby stone. An arc of pure blue light streaked from it to the contraption below which exploded in a haze of black smoke, shaking the ground beneath us.

The stranger fell to his knees before me, head bowed. When he raised his head he stared at me, open-mouthed, before asking,

"Lady, how did you do that?"

I pretended nonchalance, while I racked my brains for a suitable reply. "It was my Ruby Radium Generator," I replied.

I became aware of voices and lighted flares from a hilltop settlement behind me. Seizing my advantage, I took a moment to smooth down my clothing and tidy my hair. Drawing myself up to my full height, I said, "Why don't you take me to your leader?"

Maria Bonar

Katharine's Wild Garden

Teeming with life
native bees swarm
teeming with rain
wintering storm

A bevy of warblers
yellow-eyed currawong
precision dive-bombers
magpies' birdsong

Abundance of foliage
wind-whipped gum trees
raucous Kookaburra
scolds all that he sees

Profusion of blooms
tame and wildflowers
bedraggled, dripping
through the night hours

Tempest and thunder
night sky aflame
ruby lights strobe the
rain-streaked windowpane

Snug in the cabin
battened down, warm
alone, awake, but
safe from the storm.

Maria Bonar

Note: Written on a stormy weekend in a retreat cabin at the Katharine Susannah Pritchard Writers' Centre on Greenmount Hill.

Ruby Sunset

A little nudge was all it took to unbalance her. As usual, she disregarded the warnings. We were told not to lean over the edge of the boat but she wanted the perfect, prize-winning shot of a crocodile in the wild. Elbowing me out of the way, she tweaked the focus on her camera, but instead of her snapping the croc...

It was breathtaking how quickly the creature reared up. About three-and-a-half metres long, he leapt vertically out of the river, clamping Ruby's outstretched right arm between his jaws. She was swiftly dragged over the side, creating a tremendous splash that sent a wave washing over the deck.

All eyes were on the bride and groom making their vows at the front of the boat, their dozen guests befuddled by champagne and noonday heat. Only the vigilant young tour guide clocked the action but by then Stumpy was death-rolling Ruby underwater, taking her into the deep murk of the Adelaide River. The surface bloomed with a bouquet of blood and bubbles.

Our husbands were the first to rush over, Mike yelling, 'Somebody help! My wife's been taken by a crocodile!'

Too late, I thought. By now, Ruby probably resembled those lumps of buffalo meat the tour guide dangled over the side to entice the crocs.

Poor Mike had lost his wife. My husband, Richard, had lost his mistress. I suspected that Richard was having yet another affair with an office cutie, but it was only last night I managed to sneak a look at his iPhone while he slept in our Darwin hotel room. I was shocked to find text messages with obscene lingerie shots of my so-called best friend Ruby, revealing their sleazy liaison.

The panicked wedding guests milled around. The Captain radioed for help and the tour guide attempted to calm everyone. Ruby's hot pink fascinator suddenly shot up from the depths and floated on the blood slick, like a scene from a macabre comedy. I disguised my burst of laughter as a scream. By then everyone else was screaming and nobody paid any attention to me. As usual, Ruby managed to steal the limelight. I felt sorry for the bride being upstaged on her special day. Still, it was Eleanor's third time around and it was surely her most memorable wedding.

Maria Bonar

Sunday

iridescent wings
hover above   the koi pond

willy wagtail   dance moves
tail flashing
steals silk-wrapped bugs from cobwebs

creamy roses, pink-frilled
entice bees
to plunder their sweetness

sleepy-lidded voyeur
book abandoned
Ruby drifts on daydreams

until the iPhone's shrill clamour
propels her back to the demanding world

Maria Bonar

Mum

Remembering soft hands
Deft with needles
Skewered through
Ruby red wool
And my heart
Cry
Pause
Breathe
Remembering her mind
Razor sharp
A final
Cryptic crossword
Lying dormant
Worn and crumpled
Like my heart
Pause
Breathe
Remembering her love
Tender tattered photos
Of family
Carried close
To her heart
And mine
Breathe

Erica Bowman

Enigma

A box sits square in the middle of a round table. On it is a note which read:

Open me if you dare
For if you only sit and stare
Nothing will change
But if you open up my lid
And out-spill my content
You will at least be rid
Of curiosity.

"But curiosity killed the cat, didn't it?" was Ella's first thought, followed by "Curious is as curious does."

Ella's parents thought she was a strange little thing. Grandma too. In fact, everyone she knew had something to say about her inquisitive nature and her obsession with books.

It was the day before her 12th birthday. Ella had a suspicion that her parents had set her a trap, that this was her birthday present, which she knew shouldn't be opened until tomorrow.

Ella's thoughts were a jumble. She envisioned opening the box to find a cat hovering between life and death. Around his neck was a tag that named him "Enigma". This vision got even weirder as the cat expanded then shrunk in both live and dead forms before disappearing altogether into nothingness, whispering encouragements to open the box.

Ella blinked. The box lay unopened on the table, full of possibility.

Temptation overtook propriety. She grabbed the box, throwing off the lid. She drew in a breath as she realised the significance of the content, for inside was Grandma's ruby slippers.

She had been raised on Grandma's stories of the slippers which had transported her to another world where she had found her true self, with a little help from some friends she collected along the way.

No cats in Grandma's stories, only a little dog that accompanied her everywhere in a basket. A companion.

Ella took the slippers out of the box to try them on, but they didn't fit. They were too big. "How annoying" she thought as she picked one up, stroking it as if she could make it shrink.

If she could wear the slippers and click her heels together, maybe she too would be transported to other worlds. Maybe that would satisfy her curiosity and help her be more of herself.

At that moment, a genie appeared right in front of her. It was not your regular middle eastern, satin-and-silk type of genie. This genie was female, dressed in a red diamanté ball gown. She held what looked like a wand made of precious gems. She looked a bit frazzled and out of place.

"What do you want?" she growled at Ella.

"If I knew that," whimpered Ella, "why would I need these slippers. Why would I need you?"

The misplaced socialite was taken aback. Biting her tongue a little, she reconsidered her next words.

"There, there, dearie," she muttered. "I didn't mean to offend. It can't be that bad. Nothing a wish or two couldn't help out with, surely."

Ella thought for a moment. What was it she would have liked before she opened the box?

"I would like to be grown up," she announced, quite sure that if she had been she wouldn't have opened the box at all.

The genie-godmother tut-tutted a bit before she raised her wand, shaking it around in a kaleidoscopic frenzy before pointing it first at the box, then at the slippers before finally bringing it down, not so lightly, on Ella's head, as if to say "There! It's done!"

Ella shook her head, rubbing it with the palm of her hand to soothe the bump left behind. She noticed that the genie-godmother was nowhere to be seen. The box was back in its place. Its lid was fixed firm. It was as if it had never been opened.

She flipped the lid off without thinking. The box was empty.

She slumped on the floor and was surprised to see the slippers on her feet. They fitted perfectly, but her jeans had shrunk and were half-way up her legs. She tried to pull herself up, but her top was so tight she could hardly breathe.

It was not what she had expected. She tottered back and forth trying to gain balance, unused to wearing heels. It felt strange and awkward, but eventually she got the hang of the movement required to maintain a steady momentum and had time to have a good look around.

Everything had changed. Where there had been pictures of her on the fridge, they had been replaced with pictures of Mum and Dad looking more like Gran and Granddad.

She bit her lip. This was not what she wanted.

She felt something warm curl around her legs. She looked down to see the soft grey fur of, what she assumed was, a cat slink off down the corridor. She hurried after the creature and found it stuck in the cat flap of the back door. She opened the door and tried to pull the cat through but there was nothing there but a collar and tag.

She clicked her heels together, crying. "I want to go back to the way I was." Over and over.

It was obviously too much for the genie-godmother who appeared back on the scene.

"What is it you really want?" she uttered, shaking her head.

"I just want to be me," sobbed Ella.

"But you are, dear," whispered the magical figure, "you are."

She took the collar and tag from Ella's hand and placed it back in the box, shutting the lid firmly before waving her wand one last time.

Ella woke up and rubbed her eyes. Was it all a dream? She dressed and took herself downstairs.

Her family were waiting for her at the breakfast table with their surprise – a fluffy black kitten with a red collar and empty name tag. They were not at all surprised when she told them his name.

Aileen Boyer

Revenge is Sweet

You took the slippers
from my feet
without a thought
of me beneath
legs striped and dangling
now laid bare –
the witch is dead –
come let's all stare
and celebrate
our Dot's red shoes
her ruby feet
by Glinda fused
into her mode
of transport home
no longer doomed
to land of Oz
and scarecrow, tinman
and lion – cause
just three clicks
and she's off home
back to the farm
so far away
and I am left here
to dissolve
evaporate
into a puff of steam
as if I had never been

but I was
and will return again.

Revenge is sweet
and I will drip
each tortuous drop
beneath her feet
until she falls
and I reclaim
my ruby slippers
once again.

Aileen Boyer

Ruby Reminders

Tiny droplets gathered below the cut, ruby jewels forming on the surface before being smeared down her thigh. Jen looked away in disgust. She had no right to feel pain.

She closed her eyes, thinking of Sal. "Joined at the hip," Mum always said, but she didn't feel anything when Sal slipped away.

Jen had died inside that day. Stopped feeling.

She wondered what Sal had felt as she disappeared without even a goodbye.

Jen grabbed a cloth and wiped away the ruby remains that reminded her she was still alive, allowing pent-up tears to fall and dilute the pain.

Aileen Boyer

Strawberry Kisses

Ruby red juices
drip down her chin.
Desire rises,
she licks her lips
to catch the remnants.

Ruby red lips
form words of praise
of summer fruit.
Offerings.
Entrapments.

I catch a droplet
she has missed,
slowly wipe it away
with my finger,
which I touch to my lips

Licking the sweetness
our eyes meet
in mutual recognition
as I lean in and steal a kiss
before offering her another.

Aileen Boyer

Anniversary

'Wake up, Ruby Tuesday,' Bob sang as he placed the bouquet of red roses on the crisp white bedcover. 'Happy Anniversary, darling.'

Ruby smiled a drowsy smile, stretched and opened her soft blue eyes. 'Surely it can't be morning already? Happy anniversary to you too, dear. Oh, they're lovely,' she went on, burying her nose among the fragrant flowers.

'I've ordered us breakfast. Would you like to have it out on the balcony?'

'Oh, that would be lovely. As soon as I can get respectable.'

'You look beautiful in that,' he said, 'I'm sure the seagulls would approve. No one else is going to see you out there.'

Ruby knew that, but couldn't cope with the thought of going outside with nothing on but a filmy red nightgown, so slipped on the matching peignoir. She still hadn't recovered from the moment when she'd abandoned the frugal habits of a lifetime to buy the lovely nightwear.

A tap on the cabin door heralded the arrival of breakfast.

'Isn't this lovely," she said as they sat on the balcony, gazing out at the sunrise-gilded sea and sky.

'I'm so glad you are enjoying the cruise. Normally, I wouldn't have been game to book it without asking you. It was just when I saw the name of the ship, I knew it would be perfect. Of course, Annie encouraged me. "Go on, Dad," she said, "you and Mum have worked hard all these years and for the first time you have some real money, so go on, live dangerously, it will be perfect for your Ruby Wedding." Oh, and I bought you this too,' he went, taking a little jewellery box from his pocket.

'Close your eyes,' he said as he flipped it open to extract the ruby pendant and drape the fine gold chain around her neck.

'Oh, Bob, it's beautiful, but you must stop spending money. I know our shares are worth a lot just now, but something might go wrong.'

'Oh, stop worrying, dear. Let's just enjoy ourselves while we can. You might even get me up dancing at the final night party tonight.'

'I'll hold you to that,' she laughed.

It was a lovely day and both threw themselves into all the fun activities of cruise ship life. Looking around at all the grey heads and walking sticks, Ruby said, 'Thank you for pushing me into coming on this trip, Bobby. I'd never have agreed, you know, if you'd not dobbed me in. And it's better to come while we're young enough to make the most of it.'

Bob wasn't only a sound sleeper, he was getting deaf, so wasn't in the least disturbed by his wife's midnight sneezing attack, or noticed when she threw off the blankets and went to sit on the balcony until, chilled, she crept back into bed.

He was up first next morning, and had just finished his shower when the steward knocked on the cabin door. When Ruby didn't answer the door, he quickly wrapped a towel around his waist and emerged to collect their morning coffee.

He was surprised to see her still in bed.

'Are you okay, dear?' he asked.

'Just a bit hung-over after last night, I...' Whatever she was going to say was interrupted by a sneeze. 'I've got a terrible headache. In fact, I'm achey all over. I hope I haven't caught the flu.'

'I'll get you some paracetamol, love. And the coffee might help. Don't worry, we'll be home soon.'

Twelve months later.

'*Goodbye, Ruby Tuesday…*' the Beatles crooned as Bob and his daughter walked together along the rickety jetty, leaving the small group of friends clustered on the shore of the lake.

The creaking of the old timbers under their feet brought heart-wrenching memories of happier times spent by these waters. Ann felt the stifled sobs shaking her father's body and could no longer hold back her own tears as they reached the end of the jetty. It was time for the final act of parting.

'I don't think I can do this, Annie,' he said. 'It's so final.'

'I know, Dad, but this is where she would have wanted to be. She loved this little lake when the red-flowering gum blossoms floated like rubies on the water,' Ann said, helping him raise the urn and let the ashes gently drift down, to float away among the fallen gum blossoms.

'Oh, Annie,' he sighed, 'I don't know how I can carry on without her. It was all my fault. Oh, how I wish I'd never heard of the *Ruby Princess*.'

Lynne Cairns

Mars

Like a ruby tossed
On the night sky's velvet darkness
The red planet glows
Among the diamond stars
An innocent rust-encrusted sphere
Spinning through our galaxy

But ancient men could only see
Bloody omens in that ruddy hue
And so this innocent scarlet star
Is branded by an ancient name
Forever linked by language, myth and legend
To man's insane and genocidal game

Lynne Cairns

Menarche

The young earth spun in ecstasy
circling in the sun's red glow
to the music of the stars.
Till a stray magnetic moon,
drawing close, disturbed her dance,
Calling forth a scarlet flow
that gave the virgin Earth to know
one day she would engender life.
And as, in wonder, her spinning slowed,
ruby droplets settled on her skin
to crystallise into those glorious gems,
that hide away in secret places.

Lynne Cairns

The Magic Fruit

From her perch in the tree outside the high stone wall, the ragged girl watched with longing as the gardeners picked the luscious fruit, fruit that she, who only knew the sour berries and wizened apples that survived in the blighted wood, could not even name. Deep purple ones with soft red insides, trailing bunches of pale green berries, and round orange fruit that the men peeled to get at the strange, segmented packages of juice they slurped with pleasure. Then there were those golden globes, flushed with pink, that were carefully put aside. They were not for ordinary men she'd heard the head gardener say. They must be kept untouched for the lady and her friends, and the lord's children who came at times, wearing clothes she thought must be spun by clever magicians; silks and satins that glowed in all the colours of the rainbow, and lace as fine as spiderweb. Only they were allowed to pull and eat those golden fruit.

Dressed in her old stained homespun tunic, Asha faded into the greys and browns of the gnarled branches, so had never been noticed by the gardeners. Preoccupied with selecting the best fruit for their master, they rarely bothered to raise their eyes above the enclosing wall.

But the noble children were sometimes drawn to that other place – outside, where they had never been permitted to stray. And one small boy, examining the foreign foliage beyond the wall, was startled to see a face staring back at him.

His terrified scream, 'A goblin, a goblin!' brought the servants running, but now the older boys had seen her too.

'It's just a little one, Robin,' a big boy laughed. 'We'll soon drive it away.' Taking careful aim, he threw the pomegranate he'd just picked towards her hiding place, where it struck the branch above her with a resounding crack, releasing its red juice to splatter her face and drip into her mouth.

She should have dropped to the ground and run away, but she had never tasted anything so glorious.

Now a barrage of pomegranates descended on her and their hard shells bruised and battered the poor girl, but then one came slower, it seemed, slow enough for her to reach out and catch it.

Clutching the forbidden fruit to her chest, she slid to the ground, to scuttle away along a hidden path between the ancient trees. Eyes on the ground to avoid tripping on the great roots, it was the feet she saw first. Hardly distinguishable from those knobbly roots, they were brown, bare, dirty and knobbed with arthritis and bunions.

With her heart in her mouth, she raised her eyes. *Oh no, A forest hag!* She'd never seen one but knew immediately what it was.

'Not so fast, girl,' it growled. 'I see what you've got there and I want it. You'd better hand it over if you ever want t' see y'r ma an' pa again.'

Staring into the glowing green eyes, Asha knew she had no choice, and held out the fruit, which seemed to glow in her hand just before the hag's claws closed around it. She shuddered to hear the fruit's dying scream as it was ripped apart.

Cackling with glee, the creature scooped out the scarlet, gemlike seed sacks, crushing and squeezing them until the juice ran like blood. Then, ripping off her ragged clothes, she proceeded to spread the juice all over her skin, from head to toes.

A strange sizzling sound rent the air, and Asha watched bewildered as the ugly creature before her unravelled before her eyes then remade itself into something dazzlingly beautiful.

Shaking herself, as if to cast off any lingering hag-like remnants, this glowing being stretched to its full height, spread its beautiful arms, laughed and danced to music that seemed to come from the earth and the forest itself.

Asha fell to her knees, trembling.

'Don't grovel, girl,' the terrifying creature growled, before clearing its throat and spitting out a great glob of grey/green phlegm.

'Don't be afeared, little one,' it went on in a silvery voice. 'I did not mean to growl at you, but it annoys me how you humans think crawling around in the dirt will spare you my displeasure. But you, girl have no need to fear me. I owe you. You have restored me to myself. What gift can I give you in return?'

'Gift?' Asha squeaked.

'Yes, we immortals are empowered to grant rich rewards to mortal creatures who assist or please us.'

'But what have I done to deserve a reward?'

'You brought me the fruit. The magic fruit that held my soul entrapped. Long ago, my beauty attracted a silly, immature godling. Though I knew he held great power, I repulsed his unseemly advances and paid the price. His anger knew no bounds. He could not kill an immortal, so he ripped my soul away and trapped it in a pomegranate seed. As it grew, a magic wall grew with it. Encumbered by the crippling form of a hag, I could never hope to climb over that wall. It has been centuries and the first pomegranate tree died long ago, but I knew the magic juice would restore me if only I could obtain one. You have given me a great gift and I must reward you.'

Stooping, she scooped up a few fallen pomegranate segments, 'Look girl, see how they glow like living rubies. I can change them to those scarlet gems. As many as you like. They are worth much gold. I can make you rich.'

'My lady, thank you for the offer, but what would I do with such things. If I were found carrying jewels or gold, I would be quickly hanged as a thief. Only the nobles are allowed to have such things.'

"Well, that's an unfair arrangement. Who rules this country? I will smite them all, if that is your wish.'

'Please don't smite anyone, My Lady.'

'Well, hurry up, what reward do you want, girl? I can't hang around all day waiting.'

'I … please … if it's not too much to ask, could I have one of the trees? Those pommygranny trees that give those wonderful fruit?'

'A pomegranate? No problem about that. All the seeds dropped out when I juiced that one. See how many you can find.'

Asha squatted down to gather a handful of the black shiny seeds.

'That'll do. Here give them to me. Now, a handful of soil.'

As the girl stood up, the seeds were sprinkled into the handful of soil.

'Mix the soil with the seeds as I chant the spell of growing.'

As Asha watched in wonder, each seed sprouted a tiny green shoot, and before her eyes they all grew into small saplings.

'Well, I'll be off, then,' the lady said, beginning to fade into the green of the forest. 'Better get them home quickly before they grow too big to plant,' was the last Asha heard of her. She scooped the plants into her skirt and began to run home.

Lynne Cairns

Ruby's gifts

On Monday Ruby gave me a moon flower,
purple for tears.
On Tuesday Ruby gave me a clover,
the four leaves promising.
On Wednesday she gave me a violet,
shy as a gazelle.
On Thursday she gave me a buttercup
to hold under my chin.
On Friday Ruby gave me a feather,
enabling me to fly.
On Saturday she gave me a drop of water,
for the stillness, the sacred.
On Sunday she said,
"No more, no more, enough for now,
you have my moon, my luck,
my feelings, gold, wings and water,
all this.
No more can I give you."

Sue Clennell

Zahira

If a ruby touches a woman's skin it will grant her immediate prosperity, love and happiness (The Ancient Egyptian Pharaohs)

It is still. And silent. But that's not a bad thing. I'm overwhelmed by the beauty of my surroundings. So, this is death. The Afterlife. The relief of all my responsibilities gone is a blessing.

My long and lustrous black hair smells of Frankincense. White flowing robes of lavish quality drape my slender young body. Hands bound, palm to palm, in prayer. Between them rests a pink ruby pendant, a gift from my father.

I have always known luxury, yet it has wracked me with guilt. So many don't know it. So many poor people. My people. I have everything. But not anymore.

I'm in my burial chamber. I ask myself. *What have I learnt from this life?* Was the lesson to care for people? I tried. There were people against me. Men who wanted to stop me. I only wanted to do good things for my people. But those men had bad ways. They tried to trick me. They pretended to help the people, yet they were actually stealing from them. Food in particular.

I am sad. Yet I did my best. And now I have to leave them.

***

There was a time I was outside on a balcony. The scene exhilarating. Everybody had gathered. So many people. The heat of the day didn't deter them. A sea of olive-skinned faces. The vastness of the land a stark contrast. The masses gathered. They had come to see me.

Scared, but happy. The death of my brother, unexpected. My appointment as Pharaoh, a whirlwind of pomp and ceremony. So much responsibility weighed me down.

There were many men up here with me. But most important, a beautiful young warrior. His sole job, to protect me. He is handsome. Dark of skin. Chest bare. His muscular body a tribute to mankind. His face serene yet serious. A shaved head highlights his features. He holds a long golden spear. It is ornamental. Only used for decoration and ceremony.

There had been something between us. We liked each other. Yet I was not allowed such a dalliance. Unfortunately, he is a servant. His job to protect me. We would never be together.

I didn't know his name. Or I had never spoken it. I sensed this man loved me. A secret love. When he looked at me and smiled, my heart would melt. So handsome. And kind. My protector. That was his job.

My advisors were ridiculous. They would try to manipulate me. Tell me what to say. I tried to fight them. Disagree with them. But they connived against me. Political turmoil was rife. I had heard rumours that my gender was being blamed for the origins of our misfortunes. That I have perpetrated many sins against our nation.

I can't be sure if it is them who killed me, or I died of natural causes?

Wait. Now I recall. They didn't have the valour to kill me. They had another party execute the deed: he had no choice than to follow instructions. I am aware he had a family of his own. To not take my life he would have risked his.

The pain in my abdomen was unbearable. The spear driven through me with great force, yet I have forgiven my assassin. I was grateful for a swift death.

I will always remember my people. They were happy. They loved and rejoiced in the many festivals and celebrations of our nation. Yet so many were poor. Never enough food. The dry desert brought many challenges growing and harvesting crops. Bread and beer for the masses. Meats and wine for the privileged.

***

Inside my chamber, it is cool. A saviour from the burning heat outside. I rest, knowing I've done my best job. I have led a privileged life. My people loved me. What a handsome people they were. My heart remained pure. Many would say that to die so young was too soon. I will remain thankful for the life that I had.

I would have liked a child of my own. I had yet to marry. I kept putting it off. The choices offered by my advisors did not please me at all. In time, I would have had to agree. A male pharaoh would have many wives, even at a young age. My gender saved me from many of those expectations.

My days were pleasant. The women that served me dressed in beautiful clothing of many colours. They would dance for me in my chambers. The music hypnotic. They were like friends, but in fact servants. I would have loved to join them in the dance. But no. It would be beneath my status.

I'd never known what it was to be on my own. Even when I retired for the night. I was being protected or, was I kept from matters I should have been aware of?

Some evenings when my minder drifted off to sleep. I would venture down the corridors. Bare feet on cool tiles. Convincing myself I could go where I please. It was never long before my bravado faded and I would scuttle back to my bed chambers.

Now cool and quiet. On my own at last.

They have patched me. Wadding fills the death wound. Wadding from a sheep's fleece. It does the job. My white burial gowns guaranteed not to stain, I lie in wait for my journey to the Afterlife to begin. Fitting for the Pharaoh I am.

The grinding sound of stone-on-stone as the tomb opens. Harsh sunlight forces its way in. The servants are fearful but do as instructed.

'Remove all items of value. The gods will not grant her safe passage if she hasn't appeased them with her wealth. Be quick about it.'

They load golden goblets, jewellery and precious trinkets into hessian sacks. The tomb resealed. Quiet returns. The pink ruby remains between my palms.

Prosperity, love and happiness, will be mine…

Lucy Cotton

Ruby Anniversary

When I joined the Society of Women Writers in 1997, we met in the Blue Room opposite the State Library. The Blue Room Theatre rehearsed on the 1st Floor. It is an old building, then highly sought after for social meetings.

We crowded into a small room on the ground floor. An outside door was left open to "let in the air".

Being published in those days was rare. Many of the women did self-publish to record their story for their family. Then, as now, the room was filled with earnest seekers.

Once at the Blue Room, a display of firefighting was scheduled. All of us went out the back door to the car park area alongside. The Fire Truck drew up into the area with its crew. A fire was started in a special container and flames shot up. I did not want to take part so I retired to the rear. Many of the members were happy to take part. The firefighters gave a great display. Some members bought fire blankets.

SWW travelled to New Norcia to Retreat with Carmel Cottrell. Early on we did not go into the school buildings, the church or the monastery.

Our rooms were in the old Nun's Convent – small rooms facing onto a covered corridor – bed, wardrobe, stark white walls and ceiling. Down the corridor was a bathroom with a large, old-fashioned bathtub with a shower added above the tub. It was slippery and we took great care.

Outside, the country stretched away. The monks grew olives to make oil. There were gardens for vegetables, herbs, etc.

Once we went at 6am to the Bakery to see it in action. A monk and two helpers filled the oven. We stood back against the wall. The raw breads were loaded onto long shovels and fed into the already hot oven. Later, the oven door was opened to a swish of super-heated air and the aromatic, crisp loaves withdrawn. Some for our breakfast, some to church priests and nuns, others to be sold, even sent overseas.

Walking back to our rooms, the church bell rang. Monks came from the monastery to their church.

We walked up the hill to the school's church. Local farmers and their wives came to 7am mass.

The early sun slanted in through the upper windows. We hurried in. Were invited by those around the entrance door.

"I don't think I should go in. I'm not Catholic."

"You're a writer. Mass at 7am. Sun lights the inside of the church. Two sets of monks, chanting to each other, in Spanish, in front of a Spanish altar. If you ever want to write about any of those things, here's your opportunity."

Monks chanting across the aisle, deep, uplifting. White marble sarcophagus in the centre of the cross arms of the church. Behind, the Spanish altar defined by its vine-like design in Spanish woods.

Then we filed out, smelling the scent of frankincense.

A paddock in the centre of New Norcia has a myth of a bushfire that had threatened the town. The Abbot, Dom Salvado, obtained a painting from the church to confront the fire and the fire changed course and the buildings were saved. A small rotunda marks the spot.

In those days, laden trucks pounded through the town centre. A new highway now bypasses New Norcia.

More recently an earthquake shook Meckering leaving lines like feed thrown on the ground for cattle, of red soil. That earthquake also cracked the monastery church on the left side. If you visit, it's still apparent.

Muresk, my retreat into WA hinterland.

"Go down to the creek. You'll love it."

Years before, students from Muresk Agricultural College erected a suspension bridge across the Avon Creek.

From time to time, the creek runs at flood level. The farmers on the other side are cut off because the stream is quite fast and often carries logs of gum trees. The agriculture students needed a way to get across daily (to sheep, pigs and horses). So, the suspension bridge.

Several four or five metre tree trunks were spaced from bank to bank. They were joined by a long, thin, steel chain and wood bridge. The steel rope formed the walkway and sides, wooden slats for walking. They moved with every breath of breeze that came down the valley. Birds, corellas, lorikeets, raced by above and below. There were always birds about. The sun shone on the stones and pebbles and coarse sand. Song from the birds, whisper of breeze in the trees on both sides of the narrow creek. Keep your head up, and keep walking.

Once, walking with a fellow writer, looking across the creek:

"Look a kangaroo!"

"What? Where?"

"There."

Its glossy eyes shone as it looked at us. We eyeballed one another for a moment, then it bounded, was gone. We were surprised and awed.

Now the University students have moved on to less physical endeavours. The old suspension bridge is gated off. "Do not cross." The tree trunks are stark and staggering. The walkway is abandoned. The birds still call and fly by. We no longer go up to Muresk. R.I.P.

Time, places, people. Albany where we stayed (shhh) at the Old Quarantine Quarters, ten kilometres out of town. Kalgoorlie a magic town full of country and city people, statues and good food. Geraldton – the women pleased to be included and enjoyed.

A marching line of working women, becoming friends, some for life, exchanging thoughts and ideas. They are the shoulders we stand on. Long may we stay strong.

Leila Cue

Ruby Plums

My mother said she named me Ruby after the colour of the plums: they had a bumper crop that year. During the last stages of her pregnancy the tree was laden with pink blossom, and sure enough, after she gave birth to me the plums ripened, juicy and succulent, waiting to be devoured. When friends came to bless the baby, she gave them plums to take home. She served them plum pie with fresh cream while they sat in the garden where the tree provided shade and shelter. The tree dominated the garden where wild blackberries and rambler roses grew up the stone wall. The Victorian house in Stoke Newington, North London, had once been home to the wealthy, but all that survived from those times was a plaque in the kitchen with push buttons to summon the servants. The rich had moved to greener, outlying suburbs. In my time, it had become a working-class neighbourhood where my mother rented out the top rooms to tenants. In later years, West Indians made the area their home. But nowadays, because of its close proximity to the city, the suburb has been gentrified, the houses converted to smart apartments. Real estate agents refer to it as 'Stokey.'

Those early years are a blur, but I recall them as happy times. Our entertainment was mainly family gatherings. Sometimes we'd take a bus and ramble in the countryside. We might visit Regents Park Zoo, and afterwards in Regents Park we'd sit on deckchairs listening to the brass band playing rousing music, and breathe in the fragrance drifting from the rose gardens. Or on a fine day we'd take a steam train to South End on Sea. Once there,

I'd wade in the sea until it went out for what appeared miles, while my feet would sink into the soft squelchy mud. Later, we'd abandon the beach, taking a short train trip to the end of the pier. While walking back we'd watch a Punch and Judy show, buy fish and chips and feed the seagulls. On rainy days, we might visit the British Museum, where I learned about ancient civilisations, and prehistoric animals.

My mother read to me so I developed a vivid imagination, and my world was enhanced by the stories. I had an older brother, Don, but he didn't want to join in my 'sissy' games while I didn't care to take part in his rough and tumble activities. I had a younger, blue-eyed blond-haired brother, Martin, who was too young to play with me. My close friend was my cousin Helen who lived nearby and we played many make-believe games together. My father didn't feature too much in my life as he worked long hours as a tailor, and had another part-time job selling men's clothes in Petticoat Lane markets in the East End of London. But he'd bring home food from the markets so we'd feast on smoked salmon bagels, followed by apple strudel.

Our peace was shattered by the out-break of World War II. The relaxed atmosphere changed as my parents became worried and tense. The government issued a below ground Anderson air-raid shelter in the garden which my mother, in preparation for air-raids, furnished with a table, chairs, mattresses and tried to make it look cosy. At first, oblivious of the danger, I would spend hours playing house in it with Helen. The government informed the public that the Germans had planned a Blitz on London; the edict was that children should be evacuated to the countryside. My mother reluctantly decided she must send me and brother Don, and later Martin, away to save our lives. I felt bereft travelling on a train to an unknown destination with my name-label pinned onto my coat. We children were taken to a large hall where people chose children to take into their homes. I was one of the last to be chosen by a wealthy young couple who lived in a manor house. They didn't want a ten-year-old Jewish child in their lives; my name Ruby Cohen was a give-away. They neglected me, and went out and left me alone in the house. When my mother came to visit me, she was shocked at my condition – dirty with nits in my hair. But she found another place where I was welcomed and cared for.

When the war was over, I returned to the house in London which was still standing, although others around it were flattened. Years later, they found an unexploded bomb in the next door garden. My father who, during an air-raid, had heard a loud thump and had thought it was a chimney falling from the next door roof. Many people had been killed in the Blitz so it had been right to send the children away. Helen's parents were both killed so close family took her in, and much to my regret she moved away. We had a street party to celebrate our victory over the Germans and later when an atom bomb was dropped on Hiroshima and Nagasaki the war was finally over. We could start rebuilding our lives. We still had ration books as it was a time of austerity. Our diet included Hovis bread, plum jam, beetroot, carrots, cabbage, onions and beef mince. Children were given dietary supplements: milk, cod liver oil and malt, rose-hip syrup or concentrated orange juice, which rotted their teeth.

Winston Churchill was a wartime leader who raised the morale of the English people. What would have happened if Hitler had invaded England? As Jews, we'd have been liquidated in concentration camps. Clement Attlee was the choice for peacetime Prime Minister. He introduced the National Health Service, and other social benefits which helped the working people. Gradually life returned to normal.

The year after the war ended, the prolific plum tree produced her fruit which perhaps foretold a future of plenty. We sat in the garden, our faces dappled by the leaves of the tree which had survived the bombing and the Blitz. We drank tea from china cups and, although we had suffered both physical and emotional war damage, we had survived. I still love ruby plums, but they will never taste as sweet as they did in those halcyon days after the war was over.

Pat Curtis

Deep in the Forest

Jeb cut a track in from the main road, deep into the centre of the karri forest, and built his cabin down by the river. I told him it was dangerous digging in close to the water-line but mid-year when the river swelled with the winter rains and overflowed on the far bank, I was still able to hobble down to his trout pool and fish. I came to understand that he knew exactly what he was doing when he positioned the cabin there. He was like that, a flaming genius really. He did it all in silence too. He didn't say a word when the locals were all lining up to bag him about the dangerous material he was using for the foundations; he didn't say a word, later in the year, when his cabin was still standing high and dry, like a bird on a top branch, and those same blokes were lining up to shake his hand and tell him what a genius he was. That's the way he was though. A self-contained loner. He didn't explain himself to anyone if he didn't want to.

He'd more or less given up talking together by then. In fact, when I come to think about it, the last time I heard him say anything worth mentioning that year was at the last Anzac Day reunion when he stumbled in from the car park, his nose busted and bloody, and told everyone he was leaving. He reckoned he was going bush to surround himself with the real Australia so he'd always remember who he was and what he stood for. We all laughed. It was a bit stupid really because who we were and what we stood for was a kind of a sore point with most of us since we'd got back from Vietnam, but we laughed anyway.

That was Jeb for you. He'd make a flaming undertaker laugh sometimes. He looked around in bewilderment, his pain-filled eyes staring out from the greying red hair that covered his face like a half-closed curtain, before tangling downwards into his scruffy, white beard. Then he lay his head down on the front bar and wept. You could have cut the air with a knife then. There was no one laughing then I can tell you. He had this built-in knack of being able to silence and clear a bar quicker that anyone I knew, and there was certainly no one like him for flattening a party mood either. You might as well know, he was as mad as a cut snake, but he was ours, and a bloke would have had to be out of his mind to start laughing at him when any one of us was around. I can tell you that for sure.

So, he packed up and left town and I went with him. After all, ever since he dragged me out of that minefield near Mai Lai minus my leg and carried me back to base, we'd become inseparable. We'd been in and out of several rehabs without being rehabilitated and I guess I'd accepted that there would never be a time in my life when I would willingly part company with him. He was all that I had. My marriage had gone along with my leg and my hopes for a so-called normal type of life, and anyone I'd known before Vietnam held no interest for me and, who am I kidding, I held no interest for them either.

Life was better down south. The tall Karri trees, the cold weather and the wood fire. The smell of the wet leaves banking up against the cabin wall coaxed me out of bed each morning and eventually Jeb and I dug the land and prepared to seed a crop of corn. Then the rest of the mob arrived. I don't know about Jeb because he didn't comment, but as far as I was concerned, with them around drinking and fighting all day long, we might just as well have stayed up in Perth. Then Ruby arrived.

We all knew her. She was well known around Fremantle with her screechy voice and quirky ways but she was certainly the last person we expected to see standing in the doorway of the Pemby pub on a cold and windy night, but there she was. She looked like a wet rat with those spindly legs of hers hanging down from that brown dress she favoured. You didn't have to be a genius to see the reason it was dragging up tight across her stomach was because it was hard pressed to cover an obvious pregnancy. She was looking for Ray Donovan. He was one of ours, you know, and Bill Wylie, after banging his head up and down on the front bar several times, told her that as far as we knew he'd gone whaling down Albany way. She looked a bit put out. Then Jeb, who had been sitting near the fire, turned around and, after scratching his head for a while, told her to come over and dry herself by the fire. I nearly fell over. We all did. We looked at each other in amazement then; he asked her if she'd like a feed. She looked as stunned as we were but she shook her head slowly and continued flapping her wet dress.

'I haven't got much money, Jeb,' she said softly. 'I'll get some chips down the road.'

'Choose something from the bar menu, love,' he told her. 'I'll pick up the tab.' I nearly fell off my bar stool. Jeb never bought anything for anyone, especially women. He hated them but, as the evening went on, it became obvious that for some reason that escaped all of us, he didn't hate Ruby. We could see her puffing away on his roll your own cigarettes, something he wouldn't let anyone else do, tucking into a steak and nattering away as if there was no tomorrow and, believe it or not, Jeb was listening. It was bloody amazing. Later on, he walked out of the pub with her in tow and told us that she was coming home for the night. It was that easy for her, and she never left.

So there we all were tucked up deep in the centre of a flaming Pemberton karri forest but with the sound of Ruby's wind chimes clinking in the trees and the smell of her incense taking over the fresh air – you'd have sworn we were all back in Vietnam. It was the same eerie noise, the same sickly smell and the same feeling of fear and foreboding when we awoke to that Asian chanting she did at dawn each morning: it made us reach for our guns; it jolted and unnerved us all. I tried to have a go at her several times to give it a rest, but it never sunk in.

'A guru told me it was good for my nerves,' she said, blinking with her mouth wide open, as she slowly re affixed those hit-one-miss-one false eyelashes she wore day and night.

'It's not good for our nerves though,' I told her. She turned around quizzically.

'You don't do it though, do you?' she said, shaking her dopey head. Bill came over then. He didn't like her. That was a fact. He reckoned that he knew her intimately from Freo and that she was a right rat bag. Then there was this pregnancy business she was now fully exhibiting. She must have been six months gone if she were a day.

'Whose baby is this?' he asked. She stared at him for a moment then looked away, but when she looked back, he was still standing there.

'I'm not having a baby,' she said flatly. 'I've just put on weight.'

Bill nodded his head and smiled.

'Good one, Rube,' he said softly. 'We might be wounded but we're not brain dead, you know.' She looked away.

'I reckon it's Ray Donovan's baby,' I told him later. 'That's why she's looking for him.'

Bill nodded.

'It could be anybody's knowing her, but I've been thinking about Ray myself lately, his old lady had a baby. There was something wrong with it and it died. It busted up his marriage.' I nodded. 'I've heard that some of the other blokes have had trouble with their kids too,' he continued, 'but the main problem is that I think Jeb is thinking that the baby is his, and it's not.'

I looked at him blankly. Jeb wouldn't think that the baby was his, would he? He was a bit loopy at times but he wasn't mad and he could count, couldn't he?

'Leave her alone.' I told him. 'He seems happy enough with her and you know what he's like.' Bill nodded but I don't think he really agreed, to leave her alone, that is. She was an irritation to him. She couldn't cook to save herself and she didn't do much work around the place either. I've got to say that as far as the noise and small problems Bill extended himself more than I thought was humanly possible, for him that is. He sat her down on a number of occasions and tried to explain to her that most of the blokes had severe nerve problems, as a result of the war, and that Asian sounds and smells made us all jittery. She looked at him blankly.

'Why?' she asked with interest, rubbing her stomach. 'You're not up there anymore, you know.' Bill nodded.

'I know we're not up there anymore,' he said patiently. 'I'm not an idiot, Rube. I know where we are, but a lot of the blokes have got bad memories from when we were up there and your chanting and chimes make it worse.' She nodded her head sympathetically.

'I've got plenty of bad memories myself, Bill,' she said, nodding again, 'but I deal with them as best I can.'

I watched her from across the room. She was really mad but the extra weight was making her look better. She wore long calico dresses these days and her hair, plaited and intertwined with early wattle, looked soft and fresh, and her face looked almost gentle. Jeb looked better too. She'd cut his hair and beard and he seemed a lot more cheerful these days.

'Chanting improves tranquillity,' she was saying now. 'You should try it yourself, Bill. It might improve your mental condition.'

Time stood still then. The word mental was a trigger point of catastrophic power for Bill. He stared at her but she was rabbiting away like there was no tomorrow. It was hopeless trying to get her attention and give her the nod, because she had her eyes closed. But even if she had her eyes open, getting through to her was a long shot, and from the expression on Bill's face he was finally accepting this fact. He leapt to his feet and moved in close to her face. He told her that he was taking down the wind chimes and that if she ever put them up again or burnt one more joss stick, he was going to give her a thumping good hiding. She started to cry then and Jeb appeared. He leapt out of his wood shed like a jack-in-the-box, flew at Bill and grabbed him around the throat. They rolled down the hill punching each other with such ferocity I thought they would end up in the river. It took four of the guys to prise them apart. They'd definitely lost it. They were fighting as if they were back in Vietnam. I've never seen anything like it.

Bill moved away after that and camped further up the track. Eventually he built his own place. It was a bit of a shame really. It split the blokes up. Some of them sided with Jeb, like I did, but most of them wandered off to live with Bill, so you could say that we all had Ruby to thank for this new situation, didn't we? We'd been together all through Vietnam and we had to fall out over Ruby.

Then the baby started to come. It all began earlier than we anticipated and the sudden gush of water sent Ruby into a screeching tizz. She should have gone into town right then, like everybody else does when they have a baby. Who the hell has a baby out in the bloody forest?

It was just as well that Jeb didn't let her pursue the water birth in the flowing river business that she was on about earlier or we would have all been in dead lumber. Jeb had disappeared. He couldn't stand the stress. That left me, with one leg, trying to deliver the baby. Suddenly there was blood all over the place. One of the blokes had already run up the track to get Bill. Ruby, her face as white as paperbark was screaming as if her life was ebbing away. I was feeling sort of sick myself. Something was wrong.

You don't have to be a flaming genius to know when things are not going as they should, do you? Then the cabin door opened and Bill came in.

'What the hell's going on here?' he asked, leaning over the bed. 'What are you doing?'

'I don't know. I'm not a doctor, you know.' Bill nodded and pulled the sheet away. Ruby had her knees drawn up to her chest and Bill said that the baby's head was visible, but it looked stuck.

'Can you hear me, Rube?' he asked, softer than I had ever heard him speak to a woman before. She nodded. 'You've got to give a big push now and I'm going to try and pull it out.'

She nodded again. She seemed to get some extra strength and she hung on to his arm and pushed. He led her through it, steps by step, like a bloody champion.

Ruby lifted her head and smiled as Bill pulled the baby fully out of her body. I could hardly believe my ears when the baby cried. What a ripper! It was the best sound I had ever heard. Just seeing this new baby pop into the world sort of took my breath away. Then Bill turned it over. All the male apparatus was there but something was obviously wrong. It was his back. It was sort of twisted and there was a hole. It was really weird. The head was lopsided and its neck seemed to connect further down the back.

'Everything all right?' asked Ruby weakly, trying to sit up. I patted her back.

'Everything's fine,' said Bill, wrapping the baby in a cloth and walking over toward the door. 'You've got a boy, Rube. I'll just get Jeb.' Ruby called out that she wanted to see the baby but Bill had gone outside and closed the door.

'Lie down,' I told her. 'You've lost a lot of blood. You can bleed to death if you're not careful, you know.' There was a lot of blood and muck around and I was remembering someone saying something about getting the after-birth out. What was that?

'I'll go and see what's going on,' I said. 'You stay quiet,' and I hobbled out onto the back verandah.

'You've got to get the after birth out,' I said to Bill. 'You better come back in.'

'Don't worry about the after birth,' said Bill, holding the baby toward me.

'Look at this,' he said, pointing to the hole in the baby's back. 'I'm going to have to finish the kid off. He can't go on like this.' I stared at him in amazement.

'You can't do that,' I said, but he shrugged his shoulders and turned away.

'Don't hurt him,' said Jeb softly from the side of the verandah. We looked around. He was huddled up with his dogs as if he was one of them but he stood up now and opened his big hands toward Bill, as if he wanted the baby.

'We're going to have to do something, mate,' said Bill softly but Jeb shook his head from side to side and lumbered toward him. Ruby was screaming in the background but neither Bill nor Jeb seemed to hear her. They were struggling with each other and Bill, pushing Jeb aside with one hand, was clutching the little baby, only a few minutes old and naked and limp, in his hand, as if it were a rabbit. I'll never forget it till the day I die. Suddenly Bill broke away and, still holding Jeb back with one hand, flicked his wrist and broke the baby's neck. I nearly passed out. I've seen necks broken before. I've even broken a few myself, so I know how to do it, but to wring the neck of a little baby is something else. Jeb screamed like a mad man and lunged toward Bill and, snatching the baby from him, cradled it in his hands, and howled like a banshee. My world collapsed then. I could feel it go. I could smell the dampness of the jungle. It was as if I was in Nam again. The smell was overpowering. The crack of demolition and asbestos was all around and through the dust came Jeb, moving like the risen Christ. He was carrying an offering. I heard myself screaming. Ruby's screams were edging the background but I didn't care anymore. Bill watched me for a minute then he turned around and went back into the cabin and closed the door.

The forest is lovely in springtime. The smell of damp leaves fills the air and the winter water splashes past the rocks and tipples into the trout pool, but I don't go there anymore. None of us do. Jeb blew his brains out by that pool and I don't even want to think about it. The baby wasn't even his. I don't know how many times I tried to tell him this realistic fact but it just never seemed to sink in. Bill took me by the shoulders one night and told me that it didn't matter. He said that the baby belonged to all of us. I shrugged him away. I didn't want to hear any more rubbish. The baby might have belonged to all of them but it certainly didn't belong to me, that was for sure.

Ruby packed up and left one day when we were in town for supplies and Bill went after her. I told him it was a waste of time. I told him that she could move faster and had more places to hide than any rat I'd ever encountered. He turned on me sharply and grabbed me by the neck. His nostrils were flaring, his teeth were clenched and his eyes were solid and cold like the dead. I knew for sure then that he was going to kill me. His grip was flattening my windpipe. I was losing consciousness and at that very moment I called for my mother. Not verbally, of course, but deep in my heart I called for her. Where was Mum? I wanted to know. It was a simple request and in a flash of a second, as if by divine intervention, Bill lessened his grip. I opened my eyes. His face was close to mine. His eyes were soft but his breath was poisonous. He pulled me close to his chest, patted me on the back and told me to clean the place up. He said that she might double back. I pushed him away. I didn't need him to tell me the flaming obvious, did I? I knew that she might double back. That was just the sort of thing she would do but I needed water not a cleaning rag. Bill came in close to my face again, as if he could read my mind, and said that he'd get me some water. He said for me to rest and wait for her. He whispered in my ear that he didn't want her to come back and find us gone.

Where would we be going? I wanted to ask him that very simple question, but I thought better of it. The rest of the blokes had already left on a seek and find mission, with orders not to come back without her. They looked so purposeful when they marched away that I saluted them. Their sergeant-major shouted an order. They clicked their heels, turned their heads and saluted me back. They were the best, you know. I started to cry. My head was heavy and spinning, like the Easter Show Ferris wheel, which suddenly stopped at a realistic fact that gave some meaning to my stupid life. Whatever it was that Jeb saw in Ruby in the first place was the same thing that Bill and the others were seeing in her now.

Enid De Leo

Ruby

Thrust into the cell!
Dark and cold.
Ruby could not understand,
How her love could do this.
Her crime lactation.
Admitted to the Fremantle Asylum,
Male medical doctors called it 'puerperal madness'.
The baby would not feed at her breast,
Nor could she fulfil her wifely duties after the birth.
The year nineteen hundred and three.
Afraid and tired, she lay on the uncomfortable bed.
Would the noise ever stop?
Women cried out in anguish and fear.
Some mad, many became mad in this fortress.
The sane and mad together
How would she survive?
Did Ruby really want to?
She sobbed and stared into the dark.
Falling into a dark abyss.

Lynne Doyle

The Ticket

Parked on the roadside, Police Sergeant Con Ruby and Constable Ben Mortimer wait in the Police car for a call out.

"Holy Cow! Are we invisible? That car is moving well over a 100 k's, and that din! We'll have to give him the siren full blast."

"Right, Sarge. Wonder what his excuse will be?"

"Good morning, I am Sergeant Con Ruby. I'd like your driver's licence, sir?"

"G'day, you're on the road early. What seems to be the problem?"

"You."

"ME!?"

"You were driving well over the speed limit doing over 100 k's in a 60k zone."

"There's nobody else on the highway this hour of the morning. Fair go, mate, you're not giving me a ticket just for that."

"No."

"Good on yah. Can I go now? What are you writing?"

"Your traffic violation ticket."

"What if I tell you it's my birthday?"

"I'd say happy birthday."

"You should be out catching crooks, not writing out tickets. Is this going to take long, I'm in a hurry. I've got to sneak into the house before my wife finds out I'm missing?"

"I doubt that. Your exhaust is generating enough noise to wake up the dead."

"She's deaf. I've been meaning to get that fixed… I promise I will, Sergeant. Now can I go?"

"Not so fast. Your indicator lights aren't working. Your numberplate's coated in mud. I require you to have a breathalyser check – please blow into this tube. You're well over the limit."

"I had a couple last night – it's my birthday."

"We cannot take that into consideration."

"Look I'm in a hurry."

"I'm not. Your driver's licence please."

"Can't. My wife has it in her handbag."

"I need to inspect your vehicle. Please step out of the car?"

"No! I bleeding will not get out of my car… and you can't make me."

"I shall just add your refusal to the ticket – my constable is coming over to help you out of the car."

"He's big?"

"He is that and he will be more than happy to assist you."

"Deprivation of liberty and rights. I'll have your badge for this, Sergeant Ruby – bet your nickname is Precious, 'cause you're a real gem. I need to borrow a pen – I can't find mine."

"I'd try your wife's handbag."

"Okay, okay, I'm out. What now?"

"I'd like you to open the boot and bonnet."

"What for?"

"Routine. You have been driving under the influence and over the speed limit for starters."

"Now see here."

"I will if you open up the boot."

"Hey! Quit kicking my tyres. Is that necessary?"

"Very necessary. They have about as much tread on them as your brain."

"That's not nice. You should not speak to me like that."

"I should. You could have an accident that would cause

serious injuries, taking your life or someone else's. Let's see now … failing a breath test, unreliable indicators, number plate not visible, tyres verging on bald … that's just for starters. Now for under the bonnet."

"I can see daylight through the boot's floor, Sergeant."

"For heaven's sake! There are only a few rust holes. I place a rubber mat over them so nothing can drop through."

"I'll just have a look at the motor now."

"No need, Sarge. The engine's in an unacceptable condition. This beauty calls for a full vehicle inspection – definite yellow sticker and tow away job."

"Can I go now?"

"We'll give you a lift to the police station where you will undergo a further breathalyser test."

"Why do I need to do that again?"

"Routine, sir."

"Stuff your routine! I'll write a letter to the Commissioner of Police or what's that other fellow … 'budsman' something?"

"I think you mean the ombudsman."

"My car? I can't leave it here. Someone could nick it."

"They'd be doing you a favour."

"Some birthday! You two have spoilt my day and now you're taking my car."

"Well, sir, we're doing this so you have a positive chance of celebrating the next one. There's still a lot of day left … after you call for someone to collect you. I'm sure Constable Mortimer can rustle up a coffee and cake for you."

"I've never been in a cop car before. Doesn't your radio play music?"

"Afraid not."

"Can you turn the siren on? It's my birthday."

"I think I can arrange a couple of short blasts."

June Earle

The Will

Famous star of stage and screen, Ruby Lacompe lay supported by luxurious monogrammed cream satin pillows. A pink ribbon held sparse hair from the creased face. The flowered Saturn nightie hung on her bony physique until only the vivid blue eyes touched on the beauty she once possessed. From her ornate gilt four-poster bed, she can see framed posters of her pictures and heyday. Now well into her nineties Madam Ruby as she insists on being called summons her son Peter to come closer.

"I want to review my will."

"Mother, not now – you must rest."

"I'll rest when I'm dead. Besides, I am to receive the lead part in *Gone with The Wind.* There are matters to be sorted. Get pen and pad. Don't sigh and remove that impatient look from your face."

"Yes, Mother."

"Now, for your brother David, nothing. He's an arsehole."

"I hadn't noticed."

"Celia: she demands the chaise lounge. It's always 'Mama, I want the chaise lounge', she never stops. They presented it to me by that director, what's his name? No matter.

"So, Celia is receiving the lounge?"

"No, she's a lesbian and lesbians don't recline. I know because I used to be one."

"Shut your mouth, Peter. It is rude to gape. I don't know why children think their parents don't perform sex. Your wife Peter, gorgeous young woman, she presented me with three grandchildren. They will turn into horrors no doubt. I leave to her the washing machine, dryer, and the iron. Paula always looks so wrinkled. These will help."

"Thank you, mother. You're awfully generous."

"I know. One does what one can."

"Where is that maid? She knows I'm off to London with your father, or is that Celia's father? No matter. We're to have High Tea with the duke and duchess of something or other. I shall be late – it's unforgivable."

"Peter, I give to you the ruby and pearl necklace. You have my permission to lend it to your mistress on special occasions – just make sure you get it back. Now find that maid. We will settle this discussion tomorrow."

Sleepy, Madam Ruby drifts. Peter lays a kiss on her brow and leaves her inner sanctum. His brother and sister are awaiting in the hall.

"How is mother? Can we go in, Peter?"

"I wouldn't. She's at me to adjust her will. Celia, you're a lesbian today with your heart set on obtaining the chaise lounge. My Paula is having the washing machine, dryer and iron."

"Poor, Paula, she'll hate that. As for the chaise lounge, it's so old it probably belonged to Adam and Eve."

"How did I fare?"

"Sorry David, you're an arsehole and get nothing."

"Well, I suppose that's better than being responsible for sinking the Titanic?"

"What about you, Peter. Yesterday you had to take the French flag off the Eiffel Tower and reinstate it with the British one."

"I get the ruby and pearl necklace. If only it were real. She wore that in the ball scene in *That Lady* and it went straight back into wardrobe and props. Here comes the nurse."

"Hello, sorry I'm late. Traffic. How is Madam Ruby today?"

"You're in trouble. She's waiting to be dressed. You're off to London."

"London? I rather fancy a trip there. Yesterday we were riding camels in Morocco. In her mind, she is twenty something, and I'm in my dotage and criticised for not keeping up. By the way, did you get the will written yet again?"

"Not quite finished. On to will thirty-six. I've had writer's cramp trying to keep up with her demands."

"You are all doing so well in humouring her. Well done. Must dash. Toodle-oo as Madam Ruby says. I'll let you know how we get on in London. See you tomorrow."

June Earle

The Colour That Cannot Be Ignored

A ruby is a pink to blood-red coloured gemstone, a variety of the mineral corundum. The word ruby comes from ruber, Latin for red.

Wikipedia.

It's the award for achieving forty years of marriage, and the birthstone of those born in July. But there is more.

Nature celebrates ruby. Watch the sun rising, linger over streaks of rubescence taking over from paler colours as daylight appears. See sunsets where vermilion bleeds into the ocean.

Our balcony view of parkland with its native and exotic trees bursts into colour in October when callistemons hang out a proliferation of flame brushes.

A neighbour's geranium carries carmine blooms, and crimson roses make me think of rubies. Bird life too favours the rubine. Think of the florid flash on the wings of tropical parrots, webbed feet of some water birds.

Every day brings this colour to our notice, from traffic lights to road warnings - anything to make us aware - very much like the ruby which cannot be ignored.

None other than Nature can rival the beauty and power of
the precious stone.

And yet – in my possession is a ruby silk
scarf purchased by my mother many years ago when she saw
me admiring it in a shop window.

This I would not exchange for a priceless gemstone.

Margaret Ferrell

Rubies On Dark Velvet.

Rubies on dark velvet. A simple yet stunning window.

The display shows talent.

Your mind drifts.

One share of the plunder, yours for the taking. An echo of laughter.

Pirates sailing the seven seas. Indiana Jones, a new adventure? Or jewels stored in a forgotten tomb, fit for a King, King Solomon's mine. The dreams become fantasy, stories of treasure, Ali Baba and his forty thieves. Angry words – two men, one forces the other into a corner. A velvet bag. A pool of scarlet on the blue carpet. Murder!

You take a sideways glance. Can image your daughter saying: 'How embarrassing!' You feel foolish. Turn to walk away. Stop. Is that a body protruding from behind the showcase? You slip in. Yes, and there's splashes of blood on the counter! You stare at the floor. Snap out of it, girl! Do something! The jeweler…?

You edge forward, look around. No-one is near.

Ring an ambulance, the police?

The shop across the arcade. Did they see anything? Phone from there.

You negotiate the arcade, looking over your shoulder, back again. Where's the man? Which way did he go?

"You all right?"

Your mouth is going but there are no words. Steady girl.

"I was looking in the window ... oh never mind. The man in the shop."

You nod your head in the direction of the jeweler's. "He's

been hurt. Phone an ambulance. It looks bad."

"How bad? I mean ... shall I call the police?"

His expression screams for the whole story but he runs to the phone.

What should you do?

Now listen here, Sarah Jane, maybe you haven't been in this situation before, but stop worrying about what the family will think.

"They're on the way."

You jump. You hadn't heard the young man returning.

"Did they say what to do?" You look at your watch. "Every minute could count."

"Can I help?"

On entering the jewellers, you go straight to the victim. There's blood on his head and he is unconscious. You check for a pulse. It's weak.

You place a soft shopping parcel under his head – loosen his tie – undo the top button of his shirt, and hope it is enough. By now the young man has been told the whole story, not the bit about pirates etc., but you did mention the grey suit and the hat. He is waiting at the door for the police.

Someone grabs his arm and it's his turn to jump.

Two officers on patrol received a message from head office to confirm and call back.

An ambulance wails to a halt out the front, and a crowd begins to gather. A patrol car screeches in behind and two plain clothes detectives jump out. Not "The Untouchables", more your "Homicide" scene. Strange what you think of in moments such as these.

You've flipped, Jane would say.

The St. John's ambulance men leave with the jeweler and, after answering some questions, the young salesman returns to his job.

Déjà vu. Once more on the outside looking in. Four officers

stand in a huddle. People are staring. Do you look guilty? When you think of it…

You know what John would say: 'If I've told you once, I've told you a dozen times, never get involved.'

A forensic team is busy with powder, brushes and cameras. Your ears strain for information. Great! The jeweler has regained consciousness. Four policemen are looking in your direction. You understand in that instant why people sometimes act guilty. Once more they go over the facts.

Five feet eleven inches to six foot, approximately 180 cm, weighing around seventy-five, eighty kilos. Grey business suit, with light thin stripes; dark grey hat with brim down at the back, and dark attaché case, possibly black. You never noticed any facial features or hair colour, but got the impression it was someone in their mid-twenties. The build – movements? Something. The sergeant finishes his notes. "I think that's it for tonight."

The dimming sky, and now quiet street, make you realise the time. Your family will be worried. You should call.

"One of the officers will drive you home. Won't be long now."

The sergeant takes your hand and pumps it.

"If more people co-operated …"

You mutter something about it being okay and shift from one foot to the other.

"They're finished dusting for prints if you want to make a call."

Phone call over, and family suitably impressed. You sit down to wait. Murder she wrote – could you write about this? As officers discuss possibilities and aspects of the case, you tune in. It's starting to sound exciting.

You forget the stress, the guilt feelings, the worry and … the phone breaks your thoughts.

"Right. Good work … She's still here. Hang on. I'll ask. You sure you couldn't make an identification?"

You're still shaking your head when the phone conversation ends.

"What's happened?" You're not sure you should have asked, but why not?

"A man's been picked up at the Railway Station."

This case could be just beginning. You're excited, nervous, very caught up in the atmosphere. You should have paid more attention to detail.

A detective? You wonder. First thing tomorrow you'll make inquiries. You know you couldn't be a detective, but you could study criminology or something.

Your family? Well, right now they're still waiting for dinner. You'll cook John's favourite. Keep yourself busy. It shouldn't be more than a year or two until you find where the black markets are, where to get the best price for your lovely Red Rubies.

Marlene Fulcher

A Grandmother's Letter to God

Dear Lord,

I'm sorry to be botherin you, you so busy with all them prayers pouring in, but I'm way down at the bottom of the barrel with the strain of it all, and I'm after getting the black worry off my chest.

I'm a Protestant born and bred iffen that makes any difference. Not a devout one, I'm sorry to say, and I hope it doesn't put me right back there at the end of the line. I'm guessing them Catholics get first preference with all their pomp, rosary beads and a Pope into the bargain.

You see, Lord, my Ruby's in a tub full of trouble. Herself is like an angel, as you well know, but Lord, what in heaven's name was she doing marrying the likes of Jed Jenkins? Mind you, there's more pity in that lass's heart than most. Remember all those stray cats and dogs she took in as a child? Likely she felt sorry for the great oaf and went into weakness, but it was a thorny path she chose when she coupled with the likes of him.

Did you or the devil-incarnate fashion that frowsy son-in-law of mine? Whoever it was must have been in a mighty huge hurry or carrying a great strain on their mind. No style went into the creature's making to be sure, the clay plonked down and hacked out rough and ready.

Day after day, Himself sits on his fat derriere, guzzling the evil drink, rolling foul tobacco, and toting up the gee-gees, while his very house crumbles about him. The posts holding up the veranda where he sits will be down around his ears soon enough.

Half the house could cave in and he'd walk inside, munch his meal, and not so much as notice. Meanwhile, my Ruby's slaving her heart out to make ends meet.

I'd venture the lazy lout shoots bad seed because his daughter and two sons have inherited their fair share of wayward genes. Forgive me, Lord, but at times I wish you'd blessed my Ruby with infertility. I never felt this way till her offspring reached adolescence and the bad luck of the world descended upon us.

Rory, poor lad, isn't quite right in the head. You might say retrograde planets speckled the sky when he entered the world. Out of balance, never quite grounded, he lost his way a long time since. Took to the dope like a duck takes to water. Shaved his head and body bare, with not a hair standing, and joined a rock band. The wonder of it all was he managed to get married, and stay married for twelve months, in which time he sired twins, making me a great grandmother with many a mixed feeling. The last generation being as it is, left room for misgivings. His disgruntled wife left the nest, bairns in tow, and her ire so great she severed all connections with the family. Traumatized, Rory took to the drink along with the drugs and ended up a broke, homeless wreck till my Ruby, protector of strays, rescued him.

Unlike Rory, his brother Sean managed to be born under a lucky star. The very angels must have been smiling the day of his birth, because the lad's a veritable Adonis, so handsome he leaves the girls gasping for miles around. Tall as an ash tree, supple as a willow, his hair the colour of coal and his eyes so blue, as blue as them cornflowers growing along the wayside. It'd squeeze your heart just the look of him. Could have had his pick of the lassies, but he shied off commitment, preferred one-night-stands to a steady relationship, and it wouldn't be wondered at iffen he ended up a bachelor. All the brains in the world that lad, but like his father bone lazy. He left school to join the army and landed a cushy office job. He smoked, gambled, drank, and womanized his way to ill health and landed back on his mother's doorstep.

So, the two boys have come home to roost and their sister, Sophia, never left the nest in the first place. Too cushy and comfortable for the little madam. That one likes her comforts, to be sure, and her mother waiting on her hand and foot. Forgive me, Lord, I never thought I'd say bad things about my granddaughter, but she's like them characters I read about, a Dr Jekyll and Mr Hyde. All the signs of a split personality, she can charm you out of your wits, but if you censure or disagree with her, she turns into a she-wolf and goes for the jugular.

I don't know what the lass is playing at, but it's a dangerous game. She's tomcatting with the leader of a bikie gang. I warned her she could get pregnant or contract one of them sexual diseases. "What would you know," she spits at me. "You're just an old has-been who's probably never had an orgasm in her life."

I might not know the cat's whiskers or the organism she's on about, but I do know she's proved a trough full of grief for my Ruby, always wanting money to buy flash clothes and jewelry, all the time wanting more, more, more. So rude, but beautiful like her mother. Perhaps if she'd inherited more of her father's ugly monika her nature may have flowered differently.

Anyways, Lord, I don't know what to do. My sweet, gentle Ruby, once merry of tongue and sparkling of nature like the gemstone I named her after, is beyond herself, not knowing if she's up or down. The poor lass is fifty years old and looks a hundred. Devilish black circles under her eyes, grey in her hair and too many wrinkles too soon.

I'll venture some heathen suggestions, but I doubt they'll be acceptable in your part of the universe. Why not strike her drunken husband dead in his chair while he's quaffing his grog? A good strong lightning bolt should do it. One cheek on and one cheek off, he's sitting on hell's brink anyways.

As for my grandchildren, have them abducted by aliens who

could do experiments on their character, and send them back much the better for it.

So, I'll be saying goodbye, Lord, and sincerely hope you can help out. I've heard tell you work miracles and one's desperately needed for my precious Ruby.

Yours Respectfully,
Ellie McBride.

Robin Giraudo

The Poppy Thief

My mother never planted poppies
geraniums more her style
but poppies pink and ruby red
I cherished when a child.

Stealthily stole from other gardens
plucked silken flowers from slender stems
tucked rich booty in baggy trousers
cosseted my petal gems.

Hidden in a shoebox sturdy
underneath the house they lay
plush pink and richly red
my hijacked bright array.

When dimmed by age my gladsome gaze
falls upon poppies' rubious shades
no wish now to steal their splendor
a shoe box of treasure I remember
past poppies pink and ruby red.

Robin Giraudo

The Lighthouse

I really do not want to fall apart.
It means everything is not ok.
Thick fog continues to swirl, fades my vision.
Distorts my thoughts of Ruby
I see the lighthouse in the far distance
waiting to embrace you and guide you along.
That's when I'll be missing you.
I forgive myself for things I did not say…
That's when I'll be missing you.

Robyn Harrison

Gee

For all eleven of us grandchildren, Georgina was known simply as Gee. As the first grandchild, and only granddaughter, I like to think I was smart enough to come up with that name myself. But how? Well, G is for granny, of course! We already had a grandma and grandpa on my dad's side, so Mum's parents were supposed to be known as Granny and Grandad. But at 44 years young, Granny was too old a name for someone her age, so G for Granny it became.

My mum thinks it was more likely that I heard Grandad call her Gina, and I must have struggled to say the whole name as a child.

Either way, Gee stuck, and the ten boys followed suit. It was an ideal name in so many ways: i,t was easy to say for the young ones learning to talk, and short and simple to write. But G is for more than just Granny. She was generous with her time with us, gorgeous, gentle and glowing with health right up until the end. She was gifted with skills including sewing, and knitting, which she passed to Mum, and Mum taught me.

Her cake decorating skills were incredible. I remember hers and Grandad's ruby wedding anniversary cake. It was amazing. Gee gave us glorious food every time we visited. I can still taste her Eureka pudding with ice cream!

She was also good at badminton, and still loved the good old tunes.

In her golden years, her hair went grey, and although her mind was gone and she no longer knew who we were, her smile was genuine and she still enjoyed a giggle. On days she wasn't grumpy, that is!

There can and only will be one Gee. I will treasure my memories, until we can say G'day again. She was the greatest Gran a girl could get, for which I will always be grateful.

Gee

Melanie Hawkes

Grandad's Invention

"What are you making, Grandad?"

Ruby walks into the enormous shed, frowning at the old-fashioned phone box in the centre. Grandad steps out at the sound of her voice, wiping his hands on his overalls.

"This isn't any old phone box, you know? This is my newest invention: a teleporter!"

"A tele what?" she asks. "Have you lost your marbles?"

He laughs. "A teleporter. It allows us to travel to anywhere we like, just by entering this phone box!"

She opens her mouth and smiles. "Like Dr Who?"

"Exactly! I'm almost finished and need to test it. Where would you like to go?"

Ruby thinks for a while. "The beach!" She jumps up and down, thinking about the new bathers her grandmother bought her at the market recently.

"Alright, the beach it is. Go grab your bathers and towel. But don't tell Grandma!"

Ruby sneaks around her grandparent's house searching for her bathers while her grandad tinkers away in the shed. She grabs some chocolate-coated marshmallows for a snack too.

When she gets back to the shed, Grandad is waiting there, dressed in shorts, a t-shirt, and his hat.

"You ready, sweetie?" He takes her hand and leads her into the phone box. He shuts the door behind them and fiddles with some buttons and knobs. The phone box starts vibrating, then shaking a lot. The windows mist up and a bit of smoke enters the small enclosure. Ruby wraps her arms around her grandad's legs so she doesn't fall over, and closes her eyes.

After a few minutes, the shaking stops and she opens her eyes. They're still in the shed! "Oops, not sure what happened there!" He scratches his head.

"Are you sure it's going to work, Grandad?" Ruby is a little disappointed. It's not the first time one of his inventions has failed.

"Let me try again." He presses more buttons and pulls on more knobs, faster than last time. "Hold on tight!"

Their phone box starts swaying. Ruby holds on to her grandad's legs as tight as she can, but he falls over. They're both sitting on the floor, eyes closed, holding onto each other.

After some time, the movement stops and they open their eyes. They're in a new phone box! This one is bright red, and it's not in a dark, dirty shed. The sun is shining and Ruby can see the ocean!

Her grandad takes her hand and opens the door. "Let's go!"

They run down to the water and play in the waves. Ruby gathers shells and seaweed to show her parents when they get back. They spend hours building sandcastles and burying each other's legs.

The sun starts to set and the wind gets stronger. "Time to go, Ruby. Did you have a good time?" he asks, gathering their belongings.

"Yes, I sure did, Grandad," she replies, her smile as wide as her face. "It was marvellous!"

"Now to figure out how to get home," he mumbles to himself.

Melanie Hawkes

Score a Deal

The bell on the door jingles, waking Dennis from a lull between customers. A young woman wearing what appears to be a nurse's uniform walks in and sits down in the chair opposite.

'Welcome to Budget Travel. How may I help you?' He extends his hand across the desk; she takes it in a polite handshake. His blue uniform shirt has his name embroidered on it.

'Hi, Dennis, I need a holiday. Do you have any specials right now?'

'Do we ever! You've come to the right place. May I have your name?'

'Mary.'

'And will you be travelling alone?'

She shakes her head. 'With my husband; he's a doctor. We haven't seen much of each other due to working long hours during the pandemic. We really need a break.' She sighs and slumps back into her seat.

'Of course. How does a cruise sound, Mary?'

'A cruise?' She sits upright in her chair. 'Sounds like a slice of heaven! But aren't they expensive?'

'We've scored a deal too good to be true! Do you want to hear it?'

'Is the ocean blue? Yes, please!' She's smiling, excited to find out more.

'Well …,' he leans towards her and lowers his voice. 'The deal is you pay $1 deposit per person. The cruise is for fourteen nights, leaving from Brisbane.' He hands her a travel brochure with a picture of New Zealand on the front. 'After you come back alive and well, you pay $2,499 each.'

'$1, you say? It sounds good. When does it leave?'

'March 2023, on the ship the *Ruby Princess*.'

Mary is startled. 'Did you say the *Ruby Princess* … the ship linked to 662 cases and 28 deaths from COVID-19?'

'Yes, that's the one!' Dennis laughs. 'But don't worry, it's had a thorough clean and been disinfected. And a whole new crew will be sailing.'

'I am sure it will be fine, but still risky.' She turns the pages of the brochure, checking the details. 'What if I die on board, or soon after I return home?'

'Then you don't have to pay the rest! What do you say? Isn't it time you sprinkled some romance into your marriage and have a holiday to look forward to?'

She closes the brochure and folds it into her bag. 'I suppose you're right. Let me chat to my husband tonight.' She zips her bag closed and puts the handle over her shoulder. 'Is there a cost if we want to switch to a different ship?'

'You don't want to switch, Mary. But if you do, yes, it will cost an extra $1,000 per person.'

'Good to know.' She stands up and pushes her chair in. 'I'll call you by the end of the week to confirm. Is that ok?'

'Sure.' Dennis stands up, walks around the desk and opens the door for her. 'But hurry. At this price they're sure to sell out fast!'

Melanie Hawkes

Fudge

When Ellie was small, she spent each Saturday with her grandparents; each Saturday was the same. Her grandfather Fred, a postman, rose at four-thirty every morning so the couple habitually retired to bed in the afternoon. Saturdays and Sundays were included in this ritual, not always for sleeping, but reading, relaxing or doing the crossword.

After a busy chattering morning making fudge, treacle-toffee and cakes in the tiny kitchen, they ate lunch in the cramped dining-room where every flat surface was adorned with small brass or copper ornaments, most with engraved seaside names. For modesty's sake, Fred retired before the women, leaving Ellie and Maude to clear the table and reset it for tea.

Having lived through two world wars, depressions and rationing, Maude now enjoyed her relative prosperity regularly indulging her sweet-tooth with chocolates and sweets she had learned to make from all manner of meagre resources and as a consequence, was nearly as wide as she was tall. With a small bowl of home-made fudge from the larder to carry up to bed, Ellie stood patiently behind Maude on the narrow staircase, staring at the back of her fluff rimmed slippers while she rested, puffing and wheezing, halfway up. Sometimes Ellie gazed at the framed photographs of the young Fred in his impressive slouch hat and Anzac uniform which rose up the wall of the stairs. The four pictures portrayed his march from Melbourne through the trenches of Passchendaele to London, a handsome, laughing face at the bottom, eventually sorely wounded and bandaged in the top picture.

The small main bedroom at the top of the stairs was filled with large Victorian furniture. The double bed in the middle was high, with two sprung and one feather-down mattress. Two huge, dark walnut wardrobes, one female, one male and matching tall-boy took up two complete walls and a large dark dressing table with three-piece mirror stood in the bay window blocking most of the light. To Ellie, only just able to see over the bed, the room had the effect of walking a dark corridor, three sides of a square and definitely only one-way traffic with her grandmother in the room.

Fred's diamond-shaped knitted eye-patch and the cotton wool ball with which he padded his empty eye-socket, lay on his bed-side table. The white patch only ever came off for bed and shaving, and it was an instinctive habit of his to cover the absent eye with his hand when in company, in case it should frighten a small child or unexpected caller.

As they entered the room, Ellie climbed up on the bed beside her grandfather and tried to prise his fingers from his face to inspect the ancient war-wound.

'I dunno why you want to see it…you've seen it before!' he'd protest, until laughing he put his hand down, and let her inspect the concave sealed lids, and the deep diagonal groove in his face and hair parting formed by forty years of the patch-strings. Ellie ventured a finger to touch the eye, and at the last moment hesitated with,

'Do it 'urt, Grandad?'

'Not now it don't!' he'd chuckle, 'Did when ol' Gerry did it, by Golly!' and he'd tickle her off the bed.

Picking up the magnifying glass and recoiling his tall frame to take up just half of the bed, he returned to his book with snorting horses, cowboys and blazing guns on the cover.

One door of the largest wardrobe always stood open a few inches, and as she passed Ellie poked her head into the dark. In less happy moments, she could usually be found standing right inside the wardrobe door, fondling her grandmother's red fox fur-coat, absorbing the animal scent still prevalent over the perfume and mothballs. This was considered an undesirably sensuous habit for a little girl and her grandmother had taken to hanging the coat in differing positions at the back of the wardrobe. However, if Ellie happened to find a sleeve or piece of the hem protruding from among the dresses, she stroked it feverishly for a few precious moments, until her grandmother noticed her in the mirror.

'Leave it alone! You'll rub all the 'airs 'awf!' she'd say, struggling with her corsets in front of the dressing-table. Reluctantly closing the door, Ellie helped her grandmother unlace and unhook the complicated garment. Full spread, without the corset, Maude had a backside which put the seaside postcard ladies to shame, and Ellie play-acted that it protruded enough for her to scramble up and sit upon. Maude played along, arching her back and sticking it out even further, and they had a few giggling moments of 'bump bottoms'!

As her grandparents warmed the bed, Maude with her white curls contained in a thick blue string hair net and the *Evening News* crossword folded for action, Ellie was allowed, under a watchful eye, to play in the dressing-table centre drawer.

The ancient contents of this drawer were a little girl's delight! At the front, filled with delicate lace-edged handkerchiefs, brown oval photographs and strawberry-shaped lavender bags, still scented when pressed hard to the nose. At the back, little pinch-waist perfume bottles, score-cards for whist, and an array of pearl hat-pins. Right in the centre was a large, ornate jewellery-box filled with rings, brooches and bracelets from many generations, mostly old gold and rubies. One ruby, as big as a sixpence, was encircled with diamonds, the ring unfortunately too large for Ellie's fingers. But she liberally decorated her wrists and face with some others, and if she had been particularly good, was allowed to put on some of the bright red lipstick from the twisty-tube. When Maude wasn't looking, she added some of this to her fingernails, and putting her hands near her face, surveyed the resplendent effect of red and gold from three sides, the panorama made doubly dramatic by the twinkling reflections from the cut-glass powder-bowls and trinket trays.

Wearied at last and the powder-bowls festooned with red-smeared cotton-wool, Ellie crawled up from the foot of the bed to place herself in the middle position. A great upheaval followed, with rustling newspaper, shuffling and creaking before she could squeeze her bottom down to reach the mattress between them. When all were settled, Maude placed the bowl of fudge on the eiderdown where Ellie could reach it, and after a little prompting, started telling the story.

Always the same story, Ellie's Story, about a family of rabbits living in a wood. The baby rabbits disobeyed their mother by not staying near to the burrow as there might be foxes. Maude rustled her newspaper for dramatic effect, and in the right places paused, long and expectant, as she filled in a few squares in the crossword. At the end, the babies were pulled back in the burrow by their mother, just in time as the fox's jaws snapped shut behind them! Maude loudly clapped her hands and Ellie sank down under the covers, the fudge stuck fast in her mouth.

Her grandmother laughed at Ellie's wide eyes and wagged her finger at her saying, "And that just goes to show! You should always do what your mother tells you! Even when you're not sure why!'

After a few minutes breather and another piece of fudge, Ellie usually asked, 'Tell the story again, Nanna?'

By the second or third repeat, her grandmother began to tire, and the story was interjected with, 'What's a four-legged, hard-skinned animal, Fred? Nine letters … I don't think it's armadillo!'

This did not detract from the story. The rumbling of their

chests as they talked were the growls of the fox and the long, complicated words wafting over her head, the rustle of the trees. Ellie snuggled farther under the covers, viewing the odd twinkle from the dressing table with suspicion, craning her neck to see round the dark walnut trees. The black gap in the wardrobe doors, the faint gleam of a button, she knew he was in there somewhere!

Soon the low drone, glinting lights, the safety of the burrow, and sweet sticky fudge in her mouth, all slowly melted away.

Stella Hewson

The Ruby-Ella

The phone call came at two in the morning, shocking Jake out of his dream – another one of those where he was chasing shadows that led him nowhere. He immediately recognised Mark's voice, more frantic now than he'd ever heard from him.

"Jake! You've got to get down here."

What? At 2 in the morning, Jake thought, glancing at the clock.

"Jake! They found the Ruby-Ella!"

"What?!" Jake flung the blankets aside and started pulling jeans on over his pyjamas. It was a struggle and he peeled them back off again, the phone wedged between his shoulder and jaw. "Where? What condition is she in?"

"You won't believe this, mate … the Mamanuca Islands. She was picked up floating twenty kilometres out to sea. She's battered, but in one piece …" There was a pause, Mark waiting for Jake's next question – one he was too afraid to ask. "There was no-one in the boat, Jake."

It answered the question Jake knew better than to ask. If there'd been anyone in the boat, he'd have said they'd found Ruby and Ella.

"Sorry, mate, but at least we can trace the currents and tides and maybe pinpoint a closer location."

Jake could hear the excitement dying in Mark's voice, just as much as it was in his head. It had been six months since the dinghy had gone missing from the stern, along with his two girls during the night. He and Clara had woken just after dawn to plot the day's course to Tavua Island only to find the girls and the dinghy gone. They'd spent the day sailing around the nearby islands trying to find the tender, but nothing. Maybe they'd gone ashore to collect coconuts for breakfast – who knows what ideas a twelve and fourteen-year-old would get in their heads.

And while he knew they could handle the little Ruby-Ella that drifted behind the Clara Jay, he had serious concerns that the vessel the girls had used for years was not found floundering and that they had not been able to find it on any of the nearby shorelines of the island group they navigated through.

They had searched for days: they had radioed for assistance to search but nothing, the only thing found was one of the Ruby-Ella's oars and that off the coast of Malaysia. Eventually, he had returned home – Clara needed to be there for her chemo – this trip they'd been on probably the last for some time. What had been planned to relax her had caused her to deteriorate rapidly, her heart broken by her loss more so than the cancer ravaging her body.

The Clara-Jay had been moored up for the last three months, Jake getting on with his empty life. He had continued to sail around the islands for months after Clara's funeral, his promise to her to never give up searching. But eventually, out of necessity, he'd had to return to work – and returning to work had given him the opportunity to use the work equipment to plot locations, to ask vessels in the vicinity to keep a watch on the coastlines for signal fires or flares, to put a boat ashore for an hour or two if they could to give the girls time to reach them if they were indeed marooned.

Jake was now in his car heading to the Marine and Air Search and Rescue Centre, wondering how his boss would take it that he would again crank up the algorithms to try and narrow the search area on a search that had been dead for ten weeks. Would he have to go to war with Julia again over it?

He pulled into his parking space, flung open his door as Julia swung into her space behind him. Her door flung open as he slammed his, ready for her retribution and warnings. Snatching up her bag, she slammed her door and headed for the stairs to the front door. He would have preferred the confrontation in the car park rather than inside in front of his colleagues.

"Come on," she called to him, reefing open the heavy glass door.

Jake's heart thumped at the coming prospects, and he hurried to catch her up.

"The boat was dragging its anchor," she told him, hurrying towards the giant screens in Operations Room 3. Mark was already there; Phil too, and Dennis, all working on their calculations.

On the illuminated map on the glass table, he noted they had already placed a pin for the Clara Jay's last location where the girls had disappeared. Julia scanned the room, calculating at a glance as she always did – she had a great eye for detail.

"Don't get your hopes up, Jake, but this is looking more promising than anything we've had so far."

He was glad she didn't mention all the other possibilities that had been raised before: what if the boat had capsized? – what if the girls had gone overboard?

Jake's response was always: "they can swim and they always wore life vests." He moved over to Mark. "What was in the Ruby-Ella?" he whispered.

"Fishing gear, life vests, emergency pack, flares."

"Shit! Everything they'd need for survival."

"Doesn't matter," Julia said. "What does matter is the boat was still close to your location. As we plotted before, it should have been more towards Singapore if it was on the open sea. In six months, even close to Africa."

"In six months on the open sea," Dennis added, "it would have been swamped in a storm."

"So the girls must have made shore somewhere. They must be

on one of those islands."

Jake's heart started pounding. His girls could be alive. There was a chance!

By now Julia had spread a chart of the Mamanucas on the ops table and anchored its corners. "Look, in six months, the girls could have located help if the island was inhabited – there's resorts and regular cruise boats coming in and out on Tivua, Malalua, Molinua and Napua. But what about the uninhabited ones." She moved the paperweight to where the Clara Jay had been anchored.

Jakes's finger stabbed four islands – two to the north, two to the east. By now Phil had aerial images up on the big screen and they all stood shaking their heads – each island had a dense reef system surrounding it with minimal gaps.

"That's why they are uninhabited – it's too hard to get a boat in to land. They'd have to be one hell of a skipper … with a map … to make it to shore.

Jake's heart thudded again. *Did they hit the reef? Or run along it?* "What condition was the Ruby-Ella's hull in?" he asked.

Dennis checked his notes. "Sound as a bell, but the gunnels were badly scraped along both sides. Some gouges on the front deck canopy."

"I know they would never try and negotiate a reef. And they would *never* go out of sight of the Clara Jay. So, from where we were anchored, that leaves Monuriki and Monu islands," Jake surmised, stabbing the map with a finger.

"Both have coral reefs, and the currents are very strong," Phil pointed out, after scanning his chart information.

"Well, let's look at the current run on each," Mark suggested, zooming in on the aerial image of Monu island." A solid reef enclosed the whole land mass. "We'll come back to Monu later. Now look at Monuriki."

Jake moved closer to the screen, his gaze intense as Mark

zoomed closer in on the images of Monuriki's coastline, its surrounding reef, its sheer cliff-face on the eastern side.

"The current runs to the east," Mark added, his digital pen outlining how it would take the dinghy away from the mother vessel, away out to sea if they couldn't land the boat.

"What's that?" Jake said, pointing to the east of a white sandy shoreline.

"What?"

"What's that?" Jake now poked the screen; he turned as each of his colleagues moved closer. And Mark told him what he wanted to hear.

"It's a sea cave – probably a lava tube. Monuriki is a volcanic island."

"What if the current forced them into the cave? Could they have made it out again?"

Julia moved closer. "Lava tubes would go back into the island mass. That could be their way in."

"That would explain why no footprints on the sand. No sign of the boat," Mark added, looking at Jake.

"Why no sign of human form on the heat-seeking helicopters during our first searches," Julia added, "if they were inside the lava tubes."

"So we focus on Monuriki!"

Julia was already moving to the office. "I'll start making calls."

"I'll start getting satellite images of the island,' said Phil.

"And I'll just walk around here in circles feeling stupid," Jake murmured, still trying to convince himself his girls could be alive after six months alone on an island, and why hadn't he seen the sea cave in earlier images.

"We'd better start getting ourselves set up," Mark told him, looking brighter. "Take heart, Jake – there's hope."

Jake nodded slightly, trying to convince himself again but seeing images in his mind of the Ruby-Ella being swept into a lave tube and being choked at its throat. What if they had to bail out into the sea somewhere down its length? But if they did get out of there, they'd be okay. He'd taught them how to fish, with and without a rod; he'd taught them how to make shelters and find food –all the survival skills he'd learnt in the army. Monuriki was a nature reserve – a bird and marine sanctuary – they could have found food. They could survive on Monuriki. They could.

A smile worked its way to his lips and he scanned the screen once more, was still doing so when Julia came up behind him.

"Okay, you'd better get going. You have a flight to catch to Fiji where a rescue helicopter will fly you over the island. We'll use heat seekers first to see if we can locate them. Only if they do, will you land – the government is strict about that." But Jake was already heading out the door.

Two days later, decked out in flying suit and helmet, he scanned the thermal imaging screen, disregarding all the small pink blobs of nesting birds. What he wanted to see was larger, redder shades, shades that moved upright, that waved their arms at the aircraft.

And there it was! After two hours of grid searching the island, long red blurs, running, running into a clearing.

"Got them!" he yelled to the pilot. "Got them!" Then he remembered his Air Observer training. "Contact! One and fifty hundred metres! One o'clock!"

They swept over the location, and the giant bird lifted, turned and swung back, went into hover mode while Jake relocated them. Then Jake pointed below. "I have a visual. Two human forms." He could only hope now it was his girls and not some other lost tourists. Then tears started to well and fall as he recognised their outlines: short, dumpy Ruby, and the tall, elegant Ella. It was them!

"We can't land here," the pilot shouted across to him. "We'll fly low and slow towards the beach."

Jake watched till Ruby and Ella disappeared from sight, but they were running – running towards the beach.

An hour later, they were in his arms, looking tattered but well – Ruby somewhat slimmer, Ella more tanned – as they rapidly fired at him how they'd been swept into the cave by the strong current, how they had lived in the lava tubes in bad weather, and how the Ruby-Ella had broken her moor rope in the recent storm and drifted out of the sea cave back into the open sea.

How glad Jake was that had happened. "We'll get the Ruby-Ella back," he told them boldly, "and we'll paint her up again real fine …" anything to avoid telling them yet about their mother.

Helen Iles

To my darling wife Colleen

It's been 14,000 days my love
Give or take a few
Or 350,400 amazing hours
Each one spent with you
Sharing well over 21 million minutes
From the moment I first said I do
40 glorious years of marriage my dear
With a love that has stayed true
Even when times were hard
And winter storms blew
Together we'd get through
And whenever I feel lost my dear
I look in to your eyes of blue
To see what I always knew
That we make the perfect two

Brightly did the sun shine
On the first day that we met
It was the summer of '79
And you wore a short floral dress
Standing in the post office line
With a parcel tucked under your arm
Wrapped in brown paper and twine
You smiled at me with such charm
And asked me if I knew the time
However I was too shy to speak
Because I thought you looked divine

So you then stepped away two feet
Assuming I was a very rude lout
Which made me loudly blurt out
"11.45" with a shout

I look back on that day with a smile
After that encounter we dated a while
Then married quickly in '81
Just a few weeks out from the birth of our son
He brought us together with so much joy
And for a few happy years we cherished our boy
But then everything changed in a blink of an eye
The day sweet 6-year-old William tragically died
That was the day we almost died too
And for a while you lost me and I lost you
Grief became a mountain too steep
We parted sadly for several weeks
Until time healed our bleeding hearts
Then we moved to a new town for a fresh start
And strengthen our vow to never again part

40 years later and our love is still strong
Even on days when everything goes wrong
We have each other to weather the storms
To hold each other in sickness and keep warm
And memories we made along the way
We gathered and shared at the end of each day

I've never been a rich man and my vices are many
There are no shiny rubies or golden pennies
But together we march through thick and thin
Without fear or anger creeping in
My darling wife what else can I say
To you my love on this special day
We've seen it all you and me
And there's more to come you will see
Happy 40th Ruby Anniversary

Kate Irvine

My Dearest Frank

The years have been bitter sweet
And for many of them I did weep
But know that my heart was true
The day I wed myself to you

But we have now grown so much
And seldom dto we talk and touch
Words fall like silent snow
Our hands too are always cold

Time ticks slowly through our lives
And looking back can hurt sometimes
To reflect is to regret
Upon our ruby red sunset

But you know me
And I know you
Somehow we've made it through
A happy three that's now two

Those painful memories hurt me still
Loosing William always will
For a while I lost you
And myself in madness too

But we found a way to love again
And after forty years we're still friends
Even when the chips are down
A little luck is always found

And although we've had our ups and downs
With our smiles replaced by scornful frowns
The sun always rises the next day
To cleanse all those little worries away

We're not rich nor are we poor
We've kept the wolves outside our door
We wear no crowns or fancy jewels
But we are the merriest of fools

So my darling don't you fret
If sometimes I forget
To say those things you long to hear
After forty years I am still here

We don't need shiny rubies of red
To tell us what needs to be said
Love has endured the test of time
I'm still yours and you're still mine

So let's celebrate in our own way
And make the most of this day
As we travel down life's uncertain path
Taking the time to stop and laugh

For there have been some truly good times
So remember that and keep it in mind
Every time life throws us a hurtful spear
And takes away our shared cheer

You'll drink beer and I'll sip wine
We need no fancy place to dine
In front of the telly we'll eat tea
Steak for you and fish for me

This is what we always do
It comforts both me and you
To others our life seems mundane
But we like things to stay the same

So my love lets rise our glass
To all the years that have past
Fear not the future it's already here
And love will remain for us my dear

Kate Irvine

Mask

Ruby's mirror face screams
but her voice does not. Low moans
echo in her head, not in the empty
bedroom.

Footsteps on the stair remind her
she's not alone. The creaking door
stiffens her spine.

Mummy, where are you?

Kathleen Knight

An Anniversary Gift

Sandy and I, long-time friends, were relaxing together at a local foreshore restaurant. A glass of wine at hand, boats idly wallowing in a tranquil bay, and a sparkling ocean blending into a blue sky in the distant horizon. I found myself at peace and like all good friends we were absorbed in relaxed conversation.

After lunch, comfortable and silent in each other's company, we watched the children playing on the beach, building castles, running after beach balls and splashing in the water. Nearby, people were leisurely strolling, some with their dogs—big dogs, little dogs, cute dogs—some at nearby cafes.

"Donna, don't you have a fortieth wedding anniversary coming up soon?"

"Yes, this weekend."

"What do you think you will get from Tom? I bet you will get something special, like a diamond ring or a pearl necklace."

"Tom wants to buy me another ruby ring to commemorate our fortieth wedding anniversary. Sandy, do you remember the ring that Tom gave me as an eternity ring? Beautiful oval cut Burmese Ruby encrusted with 18 carat diamonds all around it? I loved that ring, but I lost it on the beach a few years ago. We searched for it but no luck. Tom even hired a metal detector to try to find it … but it was gone, gone for good, swallowed by the sea. I'm not sure if I want another ruby ring just yet."

"Why not?"

"I want to wait until the 'end of year' sale. The ring is outrageously expensive."

"So what's the big deal? If Tom wants to buy you a new ruby

ring, you should be happy. Besides, he can afford it. So … why such a sad face?" Sandy demanded, a tinge of surprise in her voice.

"Sandy, what I really want is something much more special. Something that would be worth much more than a ruby ring."

Sandy, intrigued, gave me one of her cheeky looks. "What can be worth more than a nice big fat ruby ring encrusted with precious diamonds?" she asked with a smirk. "Please enlighten me."

Slightly embarrassed, I warily replied, "Sandy, I know you are not going to believe me, but I wish I could have a little dog, a small puppy."

"A dog, a little dog ..." Sandy started to laugh with increasing gusto. "What's wrong with you? Are you saying you've never had a dog? Most people I know have a dog. There is nothing special about having a dog."

Frowning, Sandy continued, "I wish someone would give me a ruby ring. I would settle for a very small ruby ring without diamonds; as a matter of fact, I would settle for any ring … just give me a ring. And you … you only want a dog." Sandy started to laugh.

Sandy could not stop teasing me. She kept on giggling but I could see now that her eyes were not smiling. Sandy has never had luck with her choice of men in her life. Her last partner promised her a big diamond ring and a rose garden. She was in love and totally smitten, waiting patiently, but in the end never got what he promised her. When she found out that he was already married she was heartbroken. In tears, she booted him out of her house and out of her life.

Her next relationship was even worse. After that, Sandy virtually gave up hope of finding the right man … her soul mate with whom she could share her life with.

Somewhat clumsily, I quickly tried to change this upsetting

subject of a ruby ring.

"So, what do you think Sandy, should I get a puppy?"

"A little puppy, that's easy." Sandy responded with a smile.

"Yes, a nice little puppy with a face so adorable no one can resist, not even my husband Tom." For so long I have wanted a puppy but my husband kept dithering with the idea. To him, dogs make a lot of mess in and around the house. A mess he doesn't want to clean up!

I could see Sandy was deep in thought. "Donna, at the veterinary clinic where I work, there's a client, an old lady, Betty, who has a little Shih Tzu-Poodle cross and I know she is looking for a good home for her. She says she is too old to look after the puppy."

"Oh, really ..."

"Yes, poor woman recently had a hip operation and can hardly walk. She said her children bought her this little dog to keep her company because she lives alone."

Suddenly Sandy seemed lost for words. I kept quiet, not sure what to say.

Then, as if stirred with some new-found purpose, Sandy became animated again.

"You know, Donna, life is a *bitch*, but I am not complaining. Well, at least I have two dogs to keep me company. My two dogs are loyal, love me completely and unconditionally. Finding a right dog is easy but finding a right man is another story altogether. I gave up on my search to find a perfect man. Not everybody can get what they want or even deserve to," Sandy said with a melancholy sound in her voice.

I nodded in agreement and let her go on.

"Donna, you and Tom are so good for each other. You've been married for forty years and still love each other and that is so rare to find these days. The only thing to make your life perfect, I can now see, is that you get a dog. I'll fix that right now.

This will be my present to you for your wedding anniversary. Would you like that?"

"Of course," I responded hastily. "I'd be very grateful, but I'm not sure Tom would agree," my words trailed off to a whisper.

Sandy looked at me with a quizzical stare yet with gentle, kind and rather sad eyes. In a calm voice she asked, "How come you never had a dog? Every home needs a dog."

"Well, I did have a dog once," I said defensively, "but it was a long time ago. When I was a little girl we had a dog on our farm. He was a guard dog, protecting our chickens from prowling foxes. I loved that dog so much and we were inseparable."

My memories started flashing back. Sandy appeared intrigued so I continued.

"One moonless night two foxes came and tried to break into the hen coop. There was such a commotion, and the night was filled with screams and growls. Our brave dog stood the ground as a hero and saved all our chickens. But he died fighting those horrible foxes. I was heartbroken."

Sandy's posture and facial expression slowly changed from sympathetic to decisiveness she made a final decision.

"Donna," Sandy said firmly, "we are going to get you a dog. And we won't ask your husband for permission. As soon as I get home I'll call Betty."

"Oh no, Sandy, I need to check with Tom first. There is no point as my Tom would never agree to have a dog in the house."

Sandy gave me a disapproving look. I could sense she kind of felt sorry for me. She probably saw me as a victim of my mistaken inner beliefs and attitudes.

Slightly embarrassed, I hurriedly went on, attempting to be more convincing. This time I tried to be more logical and less emotional.

"Sandy, over the years, I've made an effort to persuade him otherwise. You know us, and you of all people should know that my dear husband can be stubborn and he doesn't like dogs. Tom was always dead set against owning a dog."

Sandy looked at me, disappointed, and said firmly, "Well it's about time that you get what you want. You have to stand up for yourself, Donna."

She went on and on about rights and obligations of spouses, how each spouse has the right to decide for themselves whether they want a pet or not.

"Tough luck for Tom!" Smiling, she said, "He'll probably be pleased because a dog is much cheaper than a ruby ring."

"But Sandy … Tom believes that having a dog would interfere with our lifestyle. We have no grandchildren. We travel as often as we please, holidays in Europe and Asia at least twice a year. Who will look after the dog?"

"Donna, stop this nonsense! I will look after your puppy, so don't worry. I will find you a perfect puppy and you will get your wish. I know Tom well enough, he will just have to get used to it. How silly this all sounds. Gosh, you only want a dog!"

After listening a bit more, I relented and agreed to get a dog without checking with my husband first. Shortly after, we parted ways, Sandy promising she would be in touch soon.

True to her word, Sandy called later that evening to tell me that Betty was happy to meet me the next day. I tried to call off our arrangement one more time but Sandy was determined and would not take no for an answer.

I reluctantly drove to Sandy's house and soon we were on our way to the old lady's house. It was love at first sight! As Betty opened her front door, the puppy, a little snow-white fur ball, slipped between Betty's legs and her walker. With a wagging tail, she snugly embraced my leg as if she would never let me go. I was suddenly excited too. *I want this little fluffy lambsy*, I thought.

The old lady spoke first. "You may not want her as she is too feisty and can never sit still. Now you can see why she is far too much for me to handle."

The little pup could not stop licking my face and my hands, and I could see that this little bundle of joy was full of effervescence and abundant energy.

Betty somewhat uneasily added, "I have to say, I'm afraid that Bon-Bon also doesn't like men."

I looked at Betty and she whispered in a soft voice, "My daughter gave me this puppy as a Christmas present so I named her Bon-Bon – French for candy because this pup is so sweet. My daughter is very busy with her new job and has no time to come for a visit. She gave me Bon-Bon as she thought that if I had a puppy to keep me company, she wouldn't have to come and visit me as often."

Betty continued talking in a soft but sad voice. "When you get to my age nobody has enough time for you. This is what old age is all about, my dear. I hope that you'll never have to find out how lonely it gets when you get old. But, such is life. No point complaining about it, nobody is listening," Betty ended her plight in a sad and resigned voice.

I felt so sorry for this poor old lady, who was struggling with her walking frame and could hardly walk. Betty was all alone, and it was quite obvious that she wasn't able to manage such a lively little puppy.

Sandy looked at me and said, "Donna, this puppy will be perfect for you. And Tom shouldn't complain because a Shih-Tzu Poodle mix is a low-maintenance dog. They are easier to manage, groom and clean up after because poodles don't shed."

Sandy waited for my response and when none came, she said in her cheeky voice, "You want her, don't you?"

I was just about to say something when Sandy picked up Bon-Bon, put her in her basket and carried the little fur-ball outside to my car. I looked at Betty's sad face and politely asked, "How much do you want for Bon-Bon?"

Betty sternly replied, "Bon-Bon is not for sale! I do not want any money for her. My Bon-Bon is worth much more than money. All I ask is that you give her love, a lot of love...because Bon-Bon's love for you will be pure and true."

Then, in her soft trembling voice, Betty said, "Sandy told me your story. I feel much better now knowing that my Bon-Bon will go to a good home where she will be loved and cared for. That is all I want for my beloved Bon-Bon."

Pausing briefly to catch a breath, Betty said, "Wait, I'll get you something you will need for Bon-Bon." She turned around and, using her walker, slowly walked away to another room. She returned with all Bon-Bon's documentation, her registration and completed vaccinations.

As we parted and said our goodbyes, I gave Betty a huge hug and promised her that her dearly loved Bon-Bon would be much loved and cared for.

As we were leaving, I insisted on paying for the vaccinations and other costs and left the money on Betty's kitchen table.

At the door, I asked Betty if she would like me to keep in touch and send her some photos of Bon-Bon, but she felt that a clean break would be much easier to handle.

In my heart, I felt sadness for poor Betty. I was suddenly struck by the plight of the aged, the forgotten people. I got into my car and looked at Bon-Bon curled up in her basket on Sandy's lap. Poor puppy; she was visibly frightened, worried and anxious, a look which said, *where are you taking me?* I gently patted Bon-Bon to reassure her.

On our way home, I thanked Sandy for such a valuable gift. I asked her if she could get some flowers for Betty on my behalf to which Sandy replied with a huge smile on her face.

"Of course, I will, my dear friend. I am so pleased that I was able to help. Good karma goes around. In the past you helped me when I needed a good friend. You are always there for me. You deserve this gift and I wish you and Tom a very happy wedding anniversary. Just be careful not to lose Bon-Bon like you did your ruby ring. Believe me, the loss of a puppy will hurt much more than the loss of a ruby ring. I suggest that you rename your puppy Ruby. That would be most appropriate. Tom wanted to buy you a new ruby, so now you have one." Sandy giggled.

I was overjoyed with her response and considered myself lucky to have such a loyal and good friend. After taking Sandy back to her house, I headed home with my new precious puppy. But the closer I got to home the more I became apprehensive. How would Tom react? Would he be pleased? What would he say? When I eventually arrived home, Tom greeted me with a worried look. Usually he got this look when I got home a bit late.

"Tom, please help me bring in our anniversary surprise gift," I asked him. "It's in my car on the front seat." Tom, still without a word, just nodded and went to the car. I watched him open the door and kept my fingers crossed. Visibly surprised, Tom just stood there looking at little Ruby. Stillness … no movement, no sound.

Then I saw a gradual transformation on Tom's face, a smile of joy, of pleasure. The moment Tom saw Ruby, her fluffy head sticking out of the basket, curiously looking up at him with puppy-dog eyes, he was transported into another world. It was love at first sight. Ruby had won him over at 'hello'. Tom gently lifted the basket and carried her into our home.

"What is her name?" Tom asked.

"Ruby," I said with a smile. "Do you like her?"

"Do I like her? I love her! I will now have two girls in my life to share my love with. She is such a precious little puppy. 'Ruby', a perfect anniversary gift for both of us."

The three of us settled down for the evening, celebrating our anniversary and sipping a glass of champagne. Every so often we would glance at our precious new gift. Ruby was sleeping peacefully in a basket next to us. Both of us realised that we now had a new family member to love and to take care of.

We cuddled up on the couch, thinking what a perfect world we live in. And yes, Ruby was the best anniversary gift we could ever wish for. I instantly forgot that I had owned and lost a valuable ruby and diamond ring. Instead, I had found a new Ruby, much more valuable than the ruby ring I'd lost. No precious stones would ever come as close to my heart as my precious little Ruby.

Over the years I often thought of Betty and wished that I could have shared some of our joys and happiness that we had with Ruby. It saddens me even now when I think of how lonely Betty was. Betty needed such a friend, a perfect companion – loyal, happy and non-judgmental. She also needed her family to care for her, but this was not to be. For some people, such as Betty, old age could be a sad and lonely existence. What a beautiful world it would be if all people had the ability to love as unconditionally as our dogs.

No wonder someone came up with this wonderful quote: 'Whoever said that diamonds are a girl's best friend … never owned a dog.' And certainly, nobody ever owned a **ruby** as beautiful as my Ruby.

Nada Lubay

Ruby the Robot

A white noticeboard stood in front of a large stone building, the signage BOTTY ROBOTS on it written in black. A red sticker stretched over it that read CLOSING DOWN.

Inside the building, Professor Botty looked at the bloody mangled mess of what had been his thumb. Then he glanced at the corner of the room where the crumpled form of the culprit lay. He sighed; he should never have attempted to use up the last spare material. His business would be closed in a few days, and his futuristic robots would cease to exist. Probably for the best after today's episode with Ruby the robot, the one lying defunct in the corner. His fingers were no longer nimble and could not manage the intricate work needed to wire and programme the robots correctly - hence the decision to close down. The demand had been so great he'd not had time to train anyone to take over.

Up until a few hours ago, his morning had passed pleasantly. People had come in to collect their orders and pay, thankful they had a robot made before he closed down.

When the door had closed behind his last customer, he hadn't bothered to lock it - there was nothing left to take. He'd made himself a cup of coffee and sat back, intending to rest before cleaning up. It was then he saw the leftover pieces of equipment. *Maybe just one more*, he thought, *before I say goodbye to all this. It can be mine.*

From the moment he started on this last model, he regretted it. He'd always been good to his robots - let them choose who they wanted to be. He even let them choose a name and decide on their own personality. So the first step was to let them speak and determine what sort of person they wanted to be in essence and, most importantly, name themselves.

He fiddled with a few wires and pressed a button that connected their voices.

"Hello, Professor Botty speaking. Tell me who you would like to be."

The robot's eyes opened, then the mouth, and it spoke. "I want to be a designer girl, a high-wired girl named Groovy."

He smiled and shrugged, definitely a little different from previous requests, but it could be done. The second step was to give them hair. He pushed another button, and black curly hair grew out of her head. Then, on a whim, he pressed her ear lobes, and long gold earrings sprang out. Now to the all-important step of connecting her name. This part needed dexterity, and this was where his problem began. It usually only took a few minutes, but his fingers slipped, fusing two wires which burped out 'RUBY is your name'.

He heard a scream from Ruby. "I wanted to be called Groovy, not Ruby!" She sank her metal teeth into his thumb, shaking it into a tangled bloody mess. "Fix it, fix it!" she yelled, yanking a large piece of his white hair out. She stood back staring at him, her hands poised, ready for attack.

He knew what was coming and tried to duck but still had to say it. "I can't because there is no reversal wire."

All his robots were programmed as individuals, and in case of a mix-up, no name could be changed. This time she attacked his beard and ripped a piece out of the side of his chin. She screamed with delight while he screamed with pain. He scrambled around the fused wires with his good fingers in the hope of finding the temporary switch off button under the mess.

She started to jig around, saying. "I won't be called Ruby. If I wanted to be a gem, I would have told you."

He was taken aback by her reasoning, secretly feeling proud

his work had progressed extensively from his prototypes: their understanding had not been modulated to answer back, except for needing any special answers from their owners in connection with their job, such as using a sensitive type of washing powder rather than the usual.

Regarding Ruby, how was this happening? His programmes and wiring did not allow for his robots to accumulate and learn worldly knowledge. The only thing he could think of was that they must have fused into a new response when the wires twisted. The fact was borne out a few minutes later - Ruby had a mind of her own. If he gave her commands to sit, she stood if he asked her to be quiet, she sang. No doubt about it, Ruby would do what she wanted.

He fumbled around the wires in desperation, trying to find a Stop button. He pressed under her arm in case a Snooze button might be there, but she countered that by raising it and socking him in the eye. He now looked a badly beaten figure, sporting a black eye, bits of his hair and beard pulled out and a mangled, bloody thumb.

He had to do something before she started on him again. Taking a lucky guess, he pressed under her big toe and found success. A Snooze button! She collapsed in a heap. He picked her up, placed her in the corner of the room until he'd attended to his thumb.

A little later, he looked over to her crumpled form. Strange to believe, but at that point, he felt sorry for her. He should never have tried to work on her when he couldn't work to the standard required. The least he could do for her was to dress her to look like the person she wanted to be.

Fossicking through one of the cupboards for an appropriate type of clothing for her, outfits he'd hired a seamstress to make, fashion not being his forte. He pulled out a jazzy sleeveless dress with a cotton headband to match. They would be perfect. *Now, how about shoes?* He sorted amongst the ladies shoes and picked out a black patent pair with a huge buckle attached. They would be ideal. *She will need accessories*, he thought and added a small handbag with a gold chain to match. Inside this, he put a bright red lipstick.

Excitement building up in him, he walked over to pick Ruby up. She would be his daughter - the demand had been so great he'd never been able to keep one of his own. But he knew that, given time and help with his stiff fingers, he could fix her bad behaviour.

He picked up her crumpled form and tenderly pulled the dress over her figure, and attached the buckled shoes to her feet. Next, he sat her up, adjusted the headband over her hair, and stretched the handbag chain over her shoulder. Her blue eyes stared out of her face. Something was missing. *Oh yes, the bright red lipstick. Wow!* With that added item, she looked startlingly beautiful. Now he needed rest before working on her, so he wandered over and put her in a spare cupboard.

On the other side of town in the Jenkins' household, the usual shouts and screams took place that morning. Bella, Mr and Mrs Jenkins' only child, was screaming, stamping her feet, and knocking chairs over. "My friends all have one! Now I want one too."

The neighbours on either side were used to it and secretly laughed at her being named Bella. "Ha, ha," said one. "I think it means beautiful, but the way she screws her face up when having tantrums, you could hardly call her that."

It didn't help when they spoke to her and said, "Good morning, Miss Want-it. How are you today? "

Today they were having a cup of tea together in one of their front gardens. "What do you think she wants this time?" said

Alice.

Joyce shrugged. "I think it might be one of those futuristic robots that will do jobs for you. A lot of children have them. But, having said that, I've heard it's closing down today ... only open for people to collect their pre-orders, so if you haven't ordered one, it will be too late."

Sure enough, a few minutes later, they saw the Jenkins leaving their house and heard the father saying to Bella, "It's no good. We can't get one - he has none left. It is only open today for pre-orders to be collected."

Bella shook her fist at them before climbing into their car, saying, "Well, he will have to find one for me somehow."

Back in his workroom, Professor Botty had finished his little rest and now picked up a broom and started the final clean up. In a few minutes, he would pick up Ruby and the spare outfits and be on his way. He was startled when the door was slammed back, and a young girl marched in, followed by an older couple.

The young girl stood and stared at him, then said, "Are you Professor Botty?"

He replied, "Yes, but I'm about to lock up and leave. Why are you here?"

She glared at him. "My name is Bella, and I'm here to get one of your robots, of course."

"Well, you can't. I've none left," he said and walked away to put the broom in the cupboard.

He watched in dismay as Bella screamed and shouted, demanding he find one. She started racing around the rooms opening cupboards and slamming them shut until finally, she opened the one containing Ruby. She grabbed her and pushed past him. "I will take this one."

He followed her to try to grab her arm and stop her, saying. "You don't understand Ruby is not finished and ..." But she evaded his grasp and raced towards the door, crying out, "She looks alright to me. Daddy, pay him!" And with that, she flounced out the door.

Professor Botty stood at the door, looking out. It had all happened so quickly. And now they were nowhere to be seen.

Shocked, he sat down at the table and cried. "My poor Ruby. Where are you now?"

As soon as Bella arrived home, she triumphantly took hold of Ruby. She started pressing her all over until, eventually, she found the button under her big toe. Ruby sat up, opened her eyes and stared at Bella.

"Where am I? Where is Professor Botty, and who are you?"

"I am Bella, your new owner, so now you belong to me."

"No, I don't," said Ruby. "I belong to Professor Botty. Where is he? He would never give me away."

Bella was taken aback at being challenged. She thought all robots took commands and followed them." Well, he didn't exactly give you to me. I found you in a cupboard and ran off with you."

Without warning, Ruby struck her on the arm. "So you are a thief!"

Bella clutched her arm and shouted, "Ouch, no! My Daddy threw money on the counter for him, and we all raced out."

Ruby yelled back. "Take me back to him, or I will hit you again!"

"I can't. He's no longer there," said Bella, shrinking back. Then, seeing the mood Ruby was in, she wrestled with her until she found the off button and pressed it.

A little later, Bella decided to take a chance and switch Ruby back on. Ruby opened her eyes. "Oh. It's you again. Please switch me off again until you find my father, Professor Botty."

"Huh, no, I won't!" said Bella. "You're mine now, and you will do what I command you to do, or I will never look for your father ever."

Ruby looked at her. "Do you know you are a mean, horrible girl?"

"No, I'm not!"

"Yes, you are."

Bella stood up and started stamping her feet and shouting. "I'm not! I'm not, but you are!"

Ruby watched her. "Not only that, but Bella means beautiful, and you are ugly. Look how you screw your face up when you're in a temper. I, too, can behave like you, but I have an excuse - I've been miswired. However, you have no excuse. My father can mend me. Perhaps your father could help you."

Disconcerted, Bella stopped stomping around and came over to her.

"What do you mean? He never stays near me."

"Not surprised," said Ruby. "Who'd want to be near you when you behave like this?"

Bella scowled, reached out and switched Ruby off.

The following morning, Bella switched Ruby back on and said, "Here are my dirty clothes. Wash them, or I will switch you off forever. I will check on you later." Then she left.

Ruby picked up the pile of clothes and went outside. *This should do it,* she thought, looking at a big muddy puddle on the drive. Without much ado, she dropped the clothes in and sloshed them around. She was about to lay them over the bushes to dry when Bella came out to check on her.

She screamed and tried to hit Ruby. "What are you doing? You've ruined my best dress?"

Ruby knocked her face down in the muddy puddle and said, "I've not been programmed yet to know how to wash clothes, but I know you need water, and that is water." She turned to go back into the house.

Bella got up from the puddle and followed her in. She yelled at Ruby and hit her.

Ruby yelled back and retaliated.

Suddenly Bella's father appeared, amazed at what was going on and tried to stop them. "What is going on here?"

"She is hitting me," said Ruby, "because I washed her clothes in a muddy puddle, but my father hasn't programmed me yet on how to do it."

To Bella's amazement, he walked over to Ruby, put his arm around her, and comforted her. "There, there, dear, it's not your fault. Let me cuddle you until you feel better."

"What about me?" Bella demanded.

He looked at her and said, "She cares she's done wrong, but you don't care about anything or anyone."

Bella stomped over and switched Ruby off.

Early the following day, Bella switched Ruby back on. "I want you to put some cream on my pancakes while I take a shower. It's a white cream in a spray can. You will find it in one of those cupboards over there." She pointed to them and left the room.

Ruby went over to the cupboards and finally found a spray can with a picture of cream on it. She headed over to the table where Bella's pancakes were lying on a plate. *Squirt, squirt.* She piled the cream all over them and returned the spray can back to the cupboard. When Bella returned, she looked at the piled-up cream and smiled: she wasn't generally allowed that much. She sat down and put a large piece of pancake in her mouth, then suddenly spat it out. She glared at Ruby.

"Ugh! What have you done to the cream? It tastes soapy." Large bubbles appeared around her mouth. "Show me the can you used."

Ruby retrieved the spray can and gave it to her. Bella read shaving cream. Taking her plate, she threw it at Ruby, splattering it all over her.

Bella's father heard the clatter and came in to see the mess. He shouted at Bella. "Come here and clean up this mess at once." Then to Bella's annoyance, he went to Ruby and tenderly started to wipe her face and clothes. Ruby clung to him. "I don't understand. I put lots of cream on."

He picked the can up and started to laugh when he read shaving cream.

Ruby said, "What's funny? I don't understand."

He explained and turned to Bella, who had now started to cry, her tears mixing with the foam. He took a towel and started to clean her face. Soothing her, holding her and giving her a cuddle. Bella loved the sensation and hugged him back.

He seemed surprised and hugged her tighter.

Later that night, Bella approached her mother and father and asked., "Mummy and Daddy, will you tuck me into bed, please?"

Shocked as they were, they replied. "We would love to."

When they had tucked her in, she snuggled down and asked, "Why haven't you done this before? I really like it."

Her mother stroked her hair. "Why? Because you've never wanted us to do it before. You always said unkind things to us and stomped off to bed afterwards."

Bella pursed her lips. "Sorry, I will try to be better."

They smiled, kissed her and said, "Goodnight, little one, we love you."

The following morning, Mr Jenkins found Bella sitting alone staring out of the window. He sat down beside her and put his arm around her. "Are you alright, Bella? You look sad? Have you switched Ruby on yet?"

She shook her head, and he saw tears in her eyes. "Hey, why not? You will get used to each other and become friends."

She started to cry. "Now I know how it feels to be loved by you. I understand how much she misses her father. I've been so mean to her."

He hugged her. "I'm pleased you understand now. He must be missing her too. We will try to contact him; he must have left a contact number."

A few days later, an important visitor knocked on the Jenkins' door. They invited him in. "Come with us, Professor Botty." They led him to a room in the back of the house and opened the door. "She's over there sitting on the chair, but she doesn't know you are coming."

Wiping the tears from his eyes, he walked over and picked her up tenderly. Then, pressing the toe button, he said, "Oh Ruby, my precious daughter, I've missed you."

Her eyes opened, and she looked at him. "Daddy, Daddy, is that really you. I've missed you so much? Please, Daddy, take me home."

"That's why I'm here," he said. "These kind people rang me and said you were unhappy and needed me to take you home, so here I am.

A short while later, they stood at the front door with the Jenkins, ready to leave. Bella stepped forward crying and kissed Ruby on her cheek. It was her way to say goodbye. Ruby stroked her, and to Professor Bottys surprise, tears ran down her face.

Professor Botty said. "You've learnt to cry. I didn't know my robots could do that."

Mr Jenkins leant forward and said, "Believe me, there has been plenty of learning going on since Ruby arrived."

Enis Pearce

To Thine Own Self Be True

The drawing-room was such a blatant display of wealth that Ruby Stirling was afraid to make any unwise movements. It suited the elegant woman who was lazily swirling the ice around in her cocktail high ball glass.

"Good evening, Mother." Ruby's soft voice caused the woman to jump, splashing droplets of cocktail. Gemma Cartier frowned as she looked up, wiping her hand with a napkin.

"Where's Bentley?"

Ruby kept her features neutral at such an abrupt greeting. "Refereeing between Papa and Dad as to which is the better football code, Aussie Rules or Soccer. You wanted to see me?" The 24-year-old didn't believe in prolonging these interactions.

"You took your time!" Mrs Cartier waved a regally bejewelled hand for Ruby to sit down.

"With Mr Rossini retiring, there's a lot of work to do before he will hand the multi-million-dollar empire over to his son." Ruby pushed a wayward red curl away from her face. The ice clinked against the glass for a moment to break the uncomfortable silence.

"Once your ridiculous job as secretary …"

"Executive Assistant," Ruby could not stop herself even though she knew her interruption would cost her dearly. This time it was just a glare.

"Soon you'll be jobless, penniless and homeless so I suppose you'll expect Enree and me to take you back in again." Gemma said "Henry" in the French manner.

Ruby shook her head, her unruly long red curls escaping from her chiffon after a long hard day. "Mr Rossini is personally interviewing future employers. I have a healthy bank balance and thanks to Papa, no student loans to pay off."

"That was a waste of a university degree! Writing."

Ruby took a deep breath and continued, "And thanks to Dad, my house in Muddy Paws Creek is mortgage free."

"Ridiculous of John! Why in some backwater little town?"

"I fell in love with Muddy Paws, it is just outside of York and only over an hour away from Perth. I've never lived in this mansion or in fact with you ever." Ruby kept her tone mild.

"You ungrateful bitch!"

"Why? Because I refused to be bullied into doing what you wanted like with my half-siblings?"

The ice cubes clinked violently. "My children are saints!"

Ruby nodded in acceptance. "I was never good enough to be considered "one of your children". Not beautiful like Sapphire."

A predatory gleam entered Gemma Cartier's eyes. "She is a socialite married to a billionaire!"

"Or smart like Diamond."

"Top plastic surgeon in Perth!"

Ruby sighed. "But not what Diamond wanted. Smart of you though, with your own plastic surgeon no one at the country club need know when you've had a touch of work done." Gemma's eyes flashed a warning but she refused to rise to the bait.

"Emerald was more power-hungry," Ruby added.

"Now the most sort after lawyer." Gemma's lips curled. "Are you still pretending to be a writer? I wonder if I should've called you after a less precious gemstone." Gemma rose and glided across to the bar to bring back the cocktail jug.

A laugh escaped from Ruby. "You called me Ruby because you got pregnant at the masquerade ball for your 40th birthday. You claim you didn't know that the man in the costume just like

Papa's that you dragged onto the balcony for sex wasn't in fact your husband. Papa forgave you, refused to let you have an abortion and even befriended Dad so that he could be a part of my life."

Gemma sank back into her chair. "You should be sinking to your knees to thank me for all I've done for you!" Ruby felt the venom dripping steadily into her veins from every strike of Gemma's fangs.

"Nearly everything I have is thanks to Papa and Dad. As soon as you gave birth you handed me to Diamond to raise along with her own son, Drew. I was only someone you could complain about to the ladies at the club."

"Everything your fathers have given you I can take away! I can take them away from you too! Ungrateful bitches get cut out of the will." The venom dug deeper, the shadows in the room became more menacing.

"Ah Cherie," said a calming voice of her 76-year-old husband from the doorway. "John and I would never agree to be parted from our daughter." Beside the Frenchman stood Ruby's 55-year-old biological father, John Stirling. He strode forward to kiss Ruby's forehead while Henry Cartier held his wife's murderous gaze.

"You're upset, Cherie, that in wanting to retire, I also desire to downsize. Sell this mansion for a penthouse. But Gemma, we talked about all the travelling we wished to do and keeping up a place this size is wasteful." Henry sat down beside his wife. "Also, I'm not going to leave everything to you, Cherie. I'm setting up substantial trust funds for all my step-children and grandchildren now. You and I will have more than enough to live on and you'll be very comfortably provided for if I predecease you."

Burning hot daggers instead of eyes looked up at her husband. "Comfortably provided? No, I earnt it all! Not some mistake that should never have been born!"

Ruby fought to not show any emotion but Henry looked extremely hurt.

"Earnt this? Is that how you see our marriage, Gemma? Is that how you saw your first two husbands? Just as ATMs?"

"Of course not!" But the answer had not come spontaneously. "I'm just rattled by your revelation after all this hellcat whining about what a bad mother I am. But, Enree, I don't want to lose face down at the club at my reduced circumstances."

John snorted. "You won't be reduced to shopping at an op shop."

Gemma cast him a glare but his words highlighted another dilemma. "All my clothes won't fit into a penthouse."

Henry laid a hand over hers. "With the clothing you know you're never going to wear again you could set up a fundraiser auctioning them for one of your charities." That seemed to please Gemma until she cast a very scrutinising glance down Ruby's curvaceous figure.

"Well, there's no point offering any clothes to the fat little secretary!"

Ruby laid a hand over John's as he was about to leap to the defence of his daughter. "There's very little call for Prada, Chanel or Louis Vuitton in Muddy Paws any way," Ruby said as calmly as she could manage.

"You'll have to give up that nonsense of living in the backwaters if you want to continue being a secretary." Gemma's venom hadn't lessened its potency yet.

Ruby dragged in a deep breath before she stated, "Actually, my dream may be about to flourish and I won't need to continue as an Executive Assistant."

Gemma scoffed. "Not your pathetic delusion to be a novelist! No one will pay to read your pointless scribbles."

Ruby glanced across at John and he smiled encouragingly. "A highly respectable publisher has offered me a contract for a series. The first book is being launched next month, the second available at Christmas. Books three and four are already in the editing mode."

John wrapped her into a bear hug. "Congratulations, sweetheart!"

Henry launched himself across the room to also embrace her. "Well done, ma petite fille!"

A harsh laugh came from Gemma. "You think you're the next J K Rowling?"

Ruby sadly shook her head. "You've always wanted me to be as good as someone else. Never about me trying to be the best me that is possible."

"If you intend to always aim low I suppose it's hard to find anything but mediocrity."

Both men began to speak in Ruby's defence but she shook her head so that she would finally defend herself.

"All my life I've quietly accepted your disapproval, your anger towards my existence and your insistence to inject poison into my veins at any opportunity. I won't accept your verbal abuse anymore. You've never once acted like a mother to me so I'll cease to call you 'Mother'. If we meet, I will continue to speak politely to you but will address you only as 'Mrs Cartier'."

The explosion was violent and yet expected. "Don't think I can't destroy this little delusion you have of making a living as an author! Your name will be so soiled you'll be right at home in your beloved Muddy Creek!"

"Non, Cherie," Henry sighed. "You'll do nothing to destroy Ruby's dreams. If she succeeds or fails it will be on her talent and not a dirty smear campaign." He glanced briefly at John who nodded in support. "I need to remind you of the pre-nuptial we signed Gemma. If I divorce you, you would walk away with very little. Don't make me choose between you and my daughter."

Gemma's cocktail went down in one long gulp. "You would never divorce me! I'm entitled to at least half of everything after all these years."

John shook his head. "You signed an infidelity clause. Our… moment on your 40th birthday would still be considered breaking that clause."

"No!" Gemma slammed the jug back down as she had been topping up her glass. "It was an accident! You forgave me! Enree, you wouldn't destroy our marriage over a mistake?" She grabbed the sleeve of her husband's jacket with real fear in her eyes. "I promise to let the career of this vile creature to crash and burn due to her own worthless talent and won't raise a hand to hasten its demise. Do you really care that much about the bitch that you would even consider threatening me with divorce?"

Henry detached the well-manicured claws from his jacket. "Oui, I have considered it, very seriously. I… this family has all been silent for far too long over your treatment of Ruby. It is time to follow my dear Mama's advice, 'If you can't say something nice, don't say anything at all'."

John chuckled. "I suppose that means you're going to be awfully silent from now on, Gemma."

The cocktail glass flew across the room and smashed against the wall, spraying an expensive painting with glass and remnants of the cocktail. Henry scrubbed a weary hand across his face as Gemma stormed out of the room.

"I'm sorry that we've never said anything before now," said Henry.

John sighed, "There could still be a fallout once Gemma has had time to think and plot."

Rising to her feet, Ruby kissed both of them on the cheek. "What can be worse than how she has treated me all these years?"

John let out a deep breath in concern. "Are you driving home tonight?"

Ruby picked up her handbag as a maid rushed in to clean up the broken glass and spilt drink. "Diamond wants me to stay with her tonight." The two men escorted Ruby to the front door.

"I'm going to the pub to watch the game and have a few beers," stated John to Henry. "You want to join me?"

Henry glanced back up at the mansion as they walked Ruby to where a car was waiting to drive her to Diamond's home.

"Who's playing?" Henry finally asked.

John chuckled as they heard a scream of outrage coming from inside the mansion. "Does it really matter?" he asked. Henry decided that it did not. Ruby hugged the two men again.

"Thank you for backing me up."

"Always enfant fille."

"It'll be all right, sweetheart," John added. "Queen Gemma just needed to be called out on her inappropriate behaviour. We'll always be there if you need us."

Sliding into the car beside her nephew, who was the same age as her, Ruby felt lighter, freer, and finally the beginning of acceptance of herself. No matter what resulted in her relationship with her mother, Ruby knew that the most important relationship she had to rebuild was with herself.

Anne Marie Price

For Ruby

Hein (rhymes with rain) died as he had lived – as an individual who made his own decisions. Hein was my neighbour, my Dutch uncle, and above all, my dear friend.

He was 95 when his carers brought him breakfast one morning and he told them, "Thank you, but no more food or drink." He had terminal cancer and was in pain, so they respected his decision and made him as comfortable as possible. Those close to him were summoned to say goodbye. He had a smile for each of us. It took him nine days to starve himself to death; this decision of his own making.

After Hein's funeral, my partner and I sat on a bench on the beachfront, watching the orange orb of the sinking sun. It seemed larger, more luminous, than previous sunsets. We found comfort in this final farewell.

"He was strong-minded," I said. "I always admired that."

My partner nodded. "Do you remember when his doctor recommended admission to the aged care home? Hein told us he had nothing in common with the others; that they were all old and herded together."

"Yes." I smiled, remembering. "He never could understand that he was also old, and needed group support. Everyone knows that!"

We both laughed. Yes, I'm so ashamed now to say we laughed. How ignorant we were and how much I have learnt since then.

Retirement, I know now that I am a retiree myself, is indeed a group thing. Somewhere around our sixty-fifth birthday, the concept of the individual dies; from that moment on, society knows better than we do what is good for us. Even those who have absolutely nothing in common will naturally thrive when finding themselves housed under one roof, fed in one room, and crowded together on coaches for group excursions. Everyone knows that!

At the heart of this problem, of course, is the fact that the word 'old' no longer engenders respect in Western culture. There are many factors at play here, but first and foremost is the belief that unless a person is earning a buck, they are redundant. Cheerful phrases such as *on the rubbish tip* and *end of life* start to crop up. Newspapers for older people necessarily include at least one page two advertisement for funerals, and an article on writing wills. Oh, and don't forget to add a couple of columns on dementia while you're at it (pun intended).

So, does it have to be like this? No, in my experience definitely not, but first you need to understand what you are up against. Stay with me and I'll give you some tips on how to survive.

When I retired, nine years ago, I allowed the group ethic to draw me in. Quite frankly, there seemed no other way. Over numerous cups of tea I listened, in frozen silence, to tales of illness, fifty-five varieties of incurable cancer, diabetes of the worst kind, deaths of relatives, friends, and public figures around the world – all over the age of 65, of course. Without realising it, I found I had joined 'the death and dying club'. At first it numbed me, then I felt myself sinking into lethargy and depression. It seemed there was no way out – until came the day that I called for help.

My doctor sent me for counselling. The psychologist I saw listened stoically to my tale of woe for half an hour, then told me the solution was in my own hands – I simply needed to 'set goals'.

"But," I gasped, "the others might not want the same thing."

"The 'others'?" he asked, raising an eyebrow.

I knew then that it was hopeless. This man was short on research; he knew nothing about retirement.

"You know, *all* of us!" I said, aware that I sounded desperate but unable to stop myself.

I could have sworn that, in this heavy moment, he smiled – but surely not.

"Ah, the group", he said. "Now there's your problem." He looked me in the eye: "To put it simply, you need to get out and get on with the job."

"But I don't have a job!" I gasped. "You don't understand. I'm a retiree!"

"Stop thinking of employment in terms of dollars," he retorted, closing his iPad with a snap. "Now, for the next few days I'd like you to become an observer: observe who is happy in retirement, and who is not. And if those around you are dragging you down, walk away. Mix with positive people. Follow your own interests. Retirement isn't a death sentence, it's just the next stage of living."

Since that time, my life has changed dramatically, as has my sense of wellbeing. My activities are varied. My friends are positive people who also avoid grouping. I assist children for whom English is their second language. I have joined a writing club, writing and publishing both a novel and a number of short stories. I am once again a film buff. And two months ago, I began an Australian Open Universities online course on creative and professional writing, thus widening my writing skills base. Part of this course requires students to write an observation portrait of someone they don't know. Without realising it initially, I hone in on someone who fits the criteria set by my former psychologist five years ago.

My focus is a grey-haired woman in my local public library, a member of the weekly Crafters' Circle. This central figure works busily at a sewing machine as the four other retirees around her chat, paying little attention to their craftwork.

I watch, unobserved, as one of the four leans across. Squinting, she picks up the packet containing patterns.

"Old-fashioned," she says, indicating the brightly coloured illustration of three dolls in different dresses. "Kids won't want these. They'll want Anna and Elsa – you know, that Disney film."

Behind the sewing machine, the woman shakes her head. "That's just the point. This is for Ruby, my granddaughter. She doesn't want her dolls looking like everyone else's."

The critic tosses the packet, turns away.

Ignoring her, the woman is busy again, trimming loose threads. The others pack up, do their leave-taking. Foot firmly on the treadle, she continues, then holds up a tiny blue doll's dress.

I clap appreciatively. She looks across, smiles. "They talk too much," she says, indicating the retreating group. "I just come to do the work."

I recognise a fellow traveller and I could say, "Join the club", but I don't. I simply nod. Like my dear friend, Hein, this woman already knows what I had to learn the hard way: that in retirement, as in each of life's stages, it's the individual, not the club, who counts.

Marilyn Rainier

Aunt Ruby

"Can you help me with these buttons?" says Aunt Ruby, my mother's youngest sister. Whitened hair lies in neat, crimped lines across her forehead. Fine-boned fingers struggle with that final elusive fastener.

Bending over her, I catch the soft lilac fragrance that is Aunt Ruby. I am filled with nostalgia for childhood. Lavender sachets for my underwear drawer, fruit bonbons, tuppeny packets of chewing gum, Aunt Ruby's face, smooth, uncreased, eyes alight with laughter, lips quirking into a smile.

So different from my mother's sternness. "Ruby was always spoilt," my mother used to mutter. "The youngest child and spoilt rotten." I'd look up at my mother's face, lips pinched tight in disapproval, frown lines scoring her brow and think, that's what I want to be – spoilt, just like Aunt Ruby.

The flutter of gossamer dresses, soft as a butterfly's wing, against milk-white skin. To my child's eyes, she was beauty, elegance, dreams. All I ever wanted was to be like Aunt Ruby.

She lived alone in a huge old house with a verandah all the way around. Its contents, gracious and olde worlde, were a constant delight to me. She let me bake scones in the huge oven of the wood stove and we laughed while she brushed flour from my cheeks and nose. We'd sit and eat the freshly buttered scones, still warm, and sip tea from tiny rose-painted China cups. I felt so grown-up and proud.

It was Aunt Ruby's shoulder I cried on when my first boyfriend let me down, her soft arms that held and soothed me, and I knew she hurt with me. You see, she hadn't always been alone. There was an old dun-coloured photograph on the mantelpiece showing a good-looking young man, with eyes that twinkled in the same way as Aunt Ruby's. His name was Ralph and several times she had told me the story of how he had gone away to war and never came back. I cried each time I heard it, holding her and burrowing my damp face into her neck.

The years passed, but Aunt Ruby was always there, like a mother, more than a mother, to me. Until suddenly I realised that Aunt Ruby was old. I hadn't noticed the silvering hair or the deepening lines near her eyes, the slight hesitancy in her gait.

Now I look at her, buttons all fastened, still-elegant feet slipped into fluffy blue slippers. Her cheeks are flushed pink and, as I take her arm to help her up, her eyes, clouded milk-white, turn towards me, unfocussed.

Guiding her between the furniture, I lead her out to the seat under the weeping willow in the garden. I sit on the grass at her feet, rest my cheek against her knee. Her hand searches, fumbles, then finds my hair and begins to stroke gently.

"Child." Her voice is soft. "Did I ever tell you about Ralphie?"

Julie Rowe

The Finest Ruby

The gemstone is extraordinary. Lying on a scrap of black velvet, its sheer magnificence makes it all but impossible to look away. The dark-suited jeweller adjusts his sleeves, flicks imaginary fluff from his coat. Clears his throat and waits, eyes down.

He has spoken passionately about the gem, inviting Andre to look more closely. "The finest ruby," he explains, "has a pure, vibrant red to slightly purplish red colour." He spreads his hands. "This ruby is gloriously red, has medium tone, vivid colour saturation and transparency. You couldn't ask for more."

Andre stoops, body slightly turned, face half-hidden. He has no idea what the jeweller is talking about. All he can see is this enchanting gem. Just like Ruby herself. He must buy it for her, nothing else is good enough. Excitement and trepidation war within. No way can he afford to buy the ruby, though desperate to do so.

How has he let it get this far? Has no idea how to extricate himself from this awkward situation. He can say he is waiting on an inheritance, except he isn't. But it's a lie that would give him an excuse to leave. Or maybe he could win Powerball, although he hasn't yet bought a ticket. Dreams and yearnings and the turmoil of his love affair have led to this moment.

A discreet cough from the jeweller pulls him back into the present. "If I could," says Andre, chagrined, "I would buy the ruby right now, this moment. But…" rubbing his hand over his face, "the reality is I need to organise my finances."

The jeweller, drawing himself to full height, expression haughty, speaks in distinct tones. "Then I suggest you do that, sir. However, I am not able to hold the ruby for you unless you are able to put down a considerable deposit." He adjusts his sleeves once more.

Andre takes his leave, embarrassed, humiliated. Sits in the car, struggling to get emotions under control. Has already forgotten what he said as he left the store. But can still see the look of disdain on the jeweller's face. He should never have ventured into the high end of town.

Must think of something, though heaven knows what. It will take a miracle for him to ever be able to afford the ruby. Pushing distressing feelings aside, he revs the car and speeds out of the car park.

A wry smile touches his lips. Hard to believe it's only eight weeks since he found the love of his life. Sighs, remembering how they first met.

He can see her now. Stunning, face alight, talking animatedly with a platinum blonde at the party. He can't recall seeing her before, was sure he would remember. Calm and cool, he strolls over, glass in hand, smiling charmingly. "Hello ladies, may I offer you a drink?" Both women turn towards him, but all he can see is the dark-haired beauty. Gives the slightest bow, "I'm Andre – at your service."

"Thanks Andre, but I'm only halfway through mine," smiles the beauty. "Kate might be ready for another one though. I'm Ruby."

Casting his mind back, he can barely remember Kate saying anything much at all, while he and Ruby talked for the remainder of the evening, interrupted only by mutual friends.

And so, the round of parties began, meeting colleagues, friends, family. Inseparable, as far as work allowed them to be. Andre showered Ruby with glorious flowers, wonderful dinners, fabulous concerts. Shouting drinks at the bar, Ruby smiling at his side. People raising their glasses, toasting him. Then, turning towards her, raising his glass again. "To my Ruby, the love of my life. I want to buy her the biggest ruby in the world!" There are laughs and groans all round.

Memories… for the short time they have been together, there are a few. A gorgeous summer day, lying on their beach towels, Andre's dark hair flopping over his forehead. Liquid brown eyes squinting against the sun's glare. Ruby lying face down, cheek resting on her hands, eyes half closed. "Have I told you why my mother called me Ruby?"

"No," he shakes his head.

"She was mad on horoscopes and I was born in July, so I'm a Cancer. And in whatever magazine she was reading, she found that the gemstone for Cancer is a ruby." She smiles. "Mum was a bit of a hippy back then and thought naming me after my birthstone was a very "in" thing to do."

Andre is fascinated. "I think I'm a Leo."

"Yes, you are."

"I'm the lion?"

"Yep, that's the one," she grins.

"Have I told you why *my* parents named *me* Andre?"

"Because they're French?"

"Partly, I suppose. But it was because it means brave and manly." He flexes his muscles. "They could tell even at birth how their son would turn out."

Ruby punches him playfully. "Did you know we're next to each other on the zodiac wheel?"

"What do you mean?"

"My birthday is in July, yours is in August, one sign follows on from the other. And you know what else?" He shrugs. "Being a Leo means you're a full-on extrovert and me being a Cancer sign means – I'm not."

"So, what's the deal there?"

"Well, I'm friendly and outgoing, to a point, but I need my time out. I love working with kids, singing, dancing, painting. Maybe I'm just a big kid." She turns onto her back.

Andre leans over and kisses her mouth. "I don't care what star signs we are, or who says what we should be. I know we're meant to be together."

"You know what's funny?" Ruby laughs. "Both star signs have no trouble falling in love fast."

"Well, I'll agree on that one." Andre rolls onto his side, throws his arm across her belly.

Weeks go by. The ruby nestles on its scrap of velvet, waiting. The non-stop party that is Andre, roars on. Until he notices that Ruby appears to have lost momentum, has an air of fragility. How could he not have noticed before?

"Rubes, are you okay?" She looks away. "What is it? What's wrong, are you sick?"

She shakes her head. "No, we do need to talk though. Can we go somewhere quiet?" Andre's heart plummets. Holds back a multitude of questions.

Sitting in the café overlooking the beach, Ruby struggles to find the right words. Finally, "I'm exhausted, Andre. I'm neglecting everybody. I think Kate's given up on me and my family hardly ever sees me." She sighs. "It's fun and I enjoy being with you and your friends, but I can't do it all the time" He, unusually, remains silent. Her forefinger traces the pattern on the tablecloth. "I know it's not easy for you to understand, because you get pumped from being around other people. I simply can't keep up." A touch of sadness in her smile. "Perhaps we're not a match made in heaven after all."

"Well, I think we are," he says softly. Andre is deeply wounded. He adores Ruby and wants to show her off to everyone, to shout it from the rooftops that she is his. She is waiting for him to say more but he remains silent.

She draws a deep breath, touch of a frown. "It was fun looking at our star signs, laughing when they said we weren't soulmates. But I've been reading a bit about which signs go together and find it depends on which websites I'm looking at. I don't know which ones are right."

"Who cares what the star signs say, Ruby! I thought we were in love. I think we're the perfect couple and the Zodiac's a load of rubbish."

Ruby sits silently. Andre wants to reach over and touch her hand or stand up and pull her to him and tell her he adores her, but she knows that already. He pushes back his chair. "Rubes, I don't know what you want. Let me know once you've decided what that is." They drive to her unit in silence. Andre hugs her tightly, kisses her cheek briefly before leaving.

He withdraws into a solitary space. Talking only when necessary, ignoring phone calls, not up for partying. He has never felt so devastated, heartbroken. It has been several weeks and he has not heard from her.

It has all been too quick, too overwhelming for Ruby. He was sure she had fallen in love with him. He made her laugh, they had fun together. She was his world but somewhere along the way he's lost her.

His sadness is palpable, his flamboyance no longer visible. Joy has fled from his eyes. He yearns to call her but has no idea how much space she needs. She has given no timeframe. And it's for her to make the next move. With a thrill of fear, he considers the possibility she may choose not to make one.

Andre sprawls in front of TV, mindlessly watching a movie he's seen at least twice before. Jumps at the unexpected blast of the doorbell. Debates whether to answer it. Doesn't feel like seeing or talking to anybody. But it rings again insistently. Mutters under his breath, shuffles to the door and drags it open.

Tears fill his eyes. Ruby stands outside, looking like her old self. Refreshed, glorious as always. "I miss you," she says.

Wordlessly, he pulls her into his arms. Her arms wind up and around his neck. "Oh, Ruby," he sighs. Kisses the top of her beautiful head.

She draws back. "Have you bought me a ruby yet?" He shakes his head. "Then don't." She presses her face against his chest. "What I'd really like is a sapphire." She smiles up at him. "Did you know that a sapphire is a ruby without the red colour?" He shakes his head again, smiling now too. "They come in a few different colours. But my favourite colour is blue."

The ruby is nestling on its scrap of black velvet, locked safely away from public view. No Powerball winnings have yet made it possible for its purchase by anyone, including Andre. But it is no longer important. The finest Ruby in the world is already his.

Julie Rowe

Seeing Green

Ruby Mason watched the grass-green ute turn in at her friend's driveway. "Yuk!" she said to Abigail. "I hate green. It's my most unfavourite colour."

"Then you'll probably hate my country cousin even more," Abigail said. She waited until the lanky twenty-four-year-old had leapt from his brand-new vehicle before introducing them. "James, meet Ruby."

"Hi," he greeted them. "Ruby? That's an old-fashioned name. What do you think of the new wheels?"

"I hate green," Ruby said, wrinkling her nose.

"Hey guys," Abigail said, "We're all friends here. James, come out the back and join the party."

James reached into the passenger side of his ute and pulled out a small package. "Hey, Cous, happy birthday," he said, handing it over.

"Thanks, James, but I said 'no presents'."

"Yeah, but I couldn't make it to your twenty-first." He grinned mischievously and winked at Ruby.

Ruby frowned. "What was that for?"

He draped an arm around her shoulders as they followed Abigail through the carport to a small rear patio. "I fancy you."

Ruby pulled away.

"He says that to all the girls," Abigail said casually. "One day he'll get lucky."

"Not today," Ruby said to both.

A dozen bodies crammed into a space designed for six made

it more intimate than Ruby felt comfortable with, especially on the impromptu dance floor. She found herself continually bumping into her friend's cousin, and each time he had a crazy remark for her.

After an hour, she'd had enough. But as she walked through the carport, he followed her.

"Not my cup of tea either. Hey, there's a movie I'd like to see while I'm in town. Want to come with me?"

She turned and glared at him. He backed off and held his hands up.

"No hanky-panky, I promise. I'd like a bit of company, that's all. I'll explode eating that huge bucket of popcorn all by myself."

Ruby laughed as she pictured him exploding. *Serve him right!*

He held the passenger's door open. With a shrug, she climbed into the garish green ute; she had nothing else planned for that weekend.

The movie was ridiculous, but they laughed at the same parts and ate too much popcorn. Afterwards, they sat in his ute outside her parents' house and talked for hours. They met again the next day, to go for a picnic and talk some more. She discovered he lived on a farm about one hundred kilometres to the south; certainly close enough to drive to the city most weekends. Before long, she was spending weekends on the farm with James and his parents.

Two years later, they married in a quaint country church. His parents moved to a small house in the town, leaving James and Ruby on the farm. It should have been the beginning of 'happily ever after', but less than six months later, his parents were involved in a serious road accident, from which his mother later died. The drought that would last for five merciless years was already beginning to affect the farm's viability. James was forced to sell all except his breeding herd for a pittance, but even that was insufficient to remain afloat.

Then Ruby suffered a miscarriage. For her, it was the final straw; farm life was too difficult to continue the struggle. She left the dying land and returned to the city to live with her parents.

James also left, landing a job in the mining industry up north to meet the farm's mortgage payments.

Just when it seemed conditions could become no worse, a bushfire sprang up. It burned through the parched land like a starving monster, devouring buildings and fences and any plant or animal not already dead.

A few days after hundreds of firefighters had finally extinguished the lethal blaze, James phoned Ruby to inform her that the farm had been burnt out, along with his father's house and half the town. He had borrowed a caravan from another cousin and moved back onto the property with his homeless father to start again. He didn't ask, but she heard the pleading in his voice to return too.

For months she ignored his unspoken message. She was living in limbo, although she tried to convince herself she was building a new life, working two casual jobs and living as much like a hermit as was possible in the same house as her concerned parents.

And then her friend Abigail married and moved to Bunbury.

"Come down for the housewarming," she invited Ruby. It was now winter, and rain had at last arrived. Ruby drove south, feeling as grey and miserable as the weather. The blackened tree trunks lining the highway seemed to be telling her this was her life now.

After a while, she noticed a flush of green along the highway verge. Fresh grass, most likely weeds, she told herself. A patch of green higher up caught her eye. A blackened trunk was sprouting new leaves! Nature was bouncing back! Could she also recover?

Ruby tried to join in the party fun at her old friend's new house, but her heart remained as cold as the wintry weather.

The next day, as she drove north, she decided to take a detour.

Just see how the farm looks now, know the worst, she told herself. Each blackened tree trunk, each burnt-out fence post, felt like another stab in her heart as she drove along a rough gravel road. But then she raised her eyes and looked across the bare paddocks past the burnt forest. A few had been ploughed by hopeful farmers, and she spotted green shoots in the furrows. She looked further away, at the unploughed, blackened land, and noticed that it too had a flush of green. The further she drove, the more she saw green in the paddocks. She arrived at the farm and pulled over.

The old farmhouse was now a pile of rubble, and further over lay a pile of twisted corrugated iron where the sheds had stood. An unburnt caravan beside it looked out of place. A small bobcat was moving around, industriously moving earth from one place to another. As she watched, it stopped and she saw James leap out. He strode over to her.

"You're back?"

She heard the hope in his voice. "Not to stay, just to look," she said, unwilling to mislead him.

"We're getting back on our feet, dad and I."

"How's he going?" she asked, concerned for his welfare. He had been devastated by his wife's death, she knew.

"Hanging in there. It's giving him something to do. Me too," he added.

She blinked back unexpected tears. "How are *you* going?"

He shrugged. "Be better with you here, but I'm managing." He turned away. "We have some of the boundary fences back up, where the neighbours are still around to help. The rubble should be cleared away soon, and then dad and I are talking about rebuilding. And we have the first dozen of a new herd coming next week, got to finish more fencing by then." He turned back to her. "What are you doing these days?"

"Still living with mum and dad. I have a couple of casual jobs to keep me out of mischief."

"There'll always be a job open here for you," he hinted.

She looked up at him, met his eyes and looked away. Could she start again?

"What made you come back?" he asked.

"The weeds were starting to grow beside the highway, and then I saw green in the paddocks."

"I remember you telling me once you hated green."

"A girl can change her mind, though I don't think it will ever be my favourite colour."

"Dad wants the new house to have a green roof."

Something in his voice made her look at him. "You're pulling my leg."

"Yep. Anything to get you back here." He smiled at her. "Although it could get crowded in the caravan."

Ruby looked across the road, seeing the rubble, but also the signs of nature regenerating in the paddocks beyond. Could their lives also regenerate? In which direction did she want her life to go? She came to a decision and started her car. "I'll be back tomorrow," she promised.

Shirley Rowland

Maroon Star Doll

Bapuji (*uncle*), Mr Bakshi, looked like a trussed goat with his arms and legs in plaster strung up with pulleys. The bandage at his fingertips, pink with blood, seemed to mock his effort to hold onto life. I felt more despair for myself than sorrow for my uncle. My resentment towards him has blinded me these last five years. Sitting here, holding my leather-bound book, I understand, and my heart is reaching out to him.

***

I, Arjun Basu, lived with my maa and baba in the outhouse of a large mansion in Calcutta. The abandoned mansion had fallen into disrepair. Families looking to escape shop doorways and plastic bags moved into habitable rooms. Soon a thriving community grew within its protective walls.

The day my life changed forever, I was waiting for maa and baba to return from Burrabazar Market. I was eager for their return, excited at their promise to buy Bengali sweets for me after I'd been diligent in my chores. A man walked into the courtyard, looked about and walked towards our home. Before he reached me, Mrs Naskar saw him; she saw everything. I was certain she had not only a third eye but a fourth one at the back of her head as well. She bustled over, asking what the stranger wanted, at the same time flapping her arms to shoo him away.

Mrs Naskar calmed as he talked and kept looking at me. The stranger stopped talking, nodded at Mrs Naskar, turned and walked away. Mrs Naskar took me to her home, where she told me my maa and baba wouldn't be coming back. A driver lost control of his bus, she explained. My maa and baba was at one of the street market stalls hit by the bus. They died along with many other people.

I stayed with Mrs Naskar until the day she told me I would be going to live with Bapuji. 'Mr Bakshi lives at Channapatna. I met him when he came to visit your maa before you were born. I thought he was a kind, gentle man. I am sure you will like your bapuji, Arjun.'

What she didn't tell me was how long the journey would be to Channapatna. Channapatna is a small village in the Bangalore district of Karnataka. Mrs Naskar put me on the train at Calcutta, where I had lived for the first ten years of my life. I left with only the clothes on my back, a small meal of rice wrapped in muslin and a bottle of water. The journey to Bangalore took a full day and a half.

Bapuji met me at the Howrah train station; he smiled at me and said, 'Welcome, Arjun, you and I will be good friends.'

I recall my dismay at the slow, long and dusty, one and a half hours it took in Mr Bakshi's old Morris Oxford to Channapatna. I tried to stay awake but sat in sullen silence. Mr Bakshi kept a wan smile on his face, neither one of us knowing what to say.

Despite my tiredness, hunger was an urgent desire when we arrived at Mr Bakshi's home. I bolted down the chicken and rice my bapuji put in front of me. I must have fallen asleep at the table as I woke the next morning on a mattress in the corner of the kitchen, with no memory of how I got there.

I lay still and quiet, seeing my maa's face smiling at me. *Up you get Arjun, off to school with you. I could hear her voice. We save paisa to make sure you get a good education, study hard, play can come later.*

Maa wouldn't let me miss school, and I didn't mind because I loved reading the history books in the school library.

My teachers fed my inquisitive brain. They would tell me, *You will go far, Arjun; we can't keep you supplied with enough books for your thirsty eyes.*

Bapuji found me on the mattress with tears on my face. The memory of my maa and baba stung and gripped my throat as I made a silent promise to apply myself to learn.

'When do I go to school, Bapuji?' I blurted.

'School? Bah!' He saw the shock on my face, 'No. You won't go to school. I will teach you all you need to know.'

I felt sparks of rage, shocked Bapuji had dismissed my maa and baba's wish.

I ate breakfast in silence.

'Come, Arjun, put away that long face. Here, my friends have given you new clothes. Hurry and get dressed. We have work to do.' Bapuji showed no heed to my sulking.

Ready, Mr Bakshi ushered me outside, announcing, 'Today, Arjun, you start to learn how to carve wood. You and I will work together.'

My anger flared. In my head I was screaming, *I want to go to school!* Consumed by anger, I didn't understand what I was seeing when I stepped over the threshold. Toys surrounded me. Confused, I stumbled further into the street; everywhere I looked I saw colourful toys.

'See, Arjun, this is where we will carve.' Bapuji touched my arm and pointed to two tables and chairs under an awning. 'This is our workshop.'

On all sides wood carved dolls, whistles and puzzles stood on crammed shelves. *How can this be, I have to work with stupid toys? Play should come later…*

I said nothing, lost in my anger and confusion, as he took my hand and led me to meet other stall vendors.

'Arjun, this is Mrs Lal. She will help you make dyes to colour the toys you make.'

Further down the street, I met Mr Mangal; he would teach me about gems and where to find them. Mr Surat was the person who would sell us our wood.

Mr Bakshi created a routine for my life around teaching me carving techniques. He gave me the choice of what to make as I learnt how to carve. I chose whistles, which I soon regretted as I broke many pieces of wood before I got the hang of carving the holes.

I visited Mrs Lal every Thursday, and she taught me how to make the dyes to paint the wood. Once every four weeks, I went with Bapuji to visit Mr Surat to buy the best wood for our work. One day my bapuji told me I would be going away with Mr Mangal for a few days to see the mineral mines of Madikari.

Mr Mangal took me to the mines where I first saw a maroon star ruby. The deep, vivid red of the gem mesmerised me.

'Arjun, why are you bobbing up and down, craning your neck at such strange angles looking at the stone?' he asked.

'Look, Mr Mangal, wherever you look at it, there is always a bright star shining from the centre.'

He laughed, 'That is how the light reflects in this precious gem, Arjun.'

Mr Mangal bought some gems. As we departed, he handed me a small bag. 'These are for you, Arjun.' He explained, 'They are small off-cuts of the maroon star ruby you were looking at. The gem cutter saw you liked the gemstone. He told me to tell you these are its children.'

And on my life rolled in the rhythm of the routine.

For five years, I kept asking Mr Bakshi to send me to school. 'Do I not give you books? Do you not learn anything here?' he would ask. My resentment grew every time he said no.

***

Yesterday, Mr Bakshi fell from a ladder. I had been holding it steady but stormed off after another refusal for me to study, leaving him alone, up the ladder. I went with him in the ambulance to the hospital and stayed with him until the doctors sent me home.

Next morning Mr Mangal roused me from sleep. 'Arjun, come tell us about your uncle.'

'Sit down, child, tell us what happened and how is your uncle?' Mrs Lal asked as she sat me on my carving stool. Mr Surat stood in the background, his arms folded, watching me with a stern look on his face.

'I left him. He refused to allow me to go to college and study,' I explained. 'Bapuji kept working; the ladder toppled as he stretched to fix the roof. He fell over the fence into the next yard and dislodged a pile of clay bricks that cascaded onto his body.'

Our three friends looked sad. I saw Mr Surat nod to Mrs Lal, then Mr Mangal gave her a curt nod.

'Today is your fifteenth birthday, Arjun?' Mrs Lal asked. I nodded, and she continued, 'Your uncle gave me this so you wouldn't see it before today. Take it.'

She handed me a sandalwood box, its surface covered by the intricate carved design of a large building. 'Open it, Arjun,' she coaxed.

Inside the box was a leather-bound book and a pen. I picked up the book, perplexed when I flicked the pages and saw they were blank. A folded piece of paper fell onto my lap. I read it and asked, 'But what does this mean?'

Mr Surat was gruff when he spoke first. 'Have I not taught you about the history of the Persian artisans? Do you not know of the traditional ivory-wood they introduced to our forefathers? Do you not know where to find the best rosewood and sandalwood in India? Bah.'

Mr Mangal sounded exasperated. 'Have I not taught you about minerals and gemstones? Do you not understand about the subtleties of rock formation? Or where to find precious stones in India and other countries?'

'What about the vegetables?' Mrs Lal spoke in a quiet but

insistent voice. 'Their special qualities in making colourful dyes? Do you recall our many conversations about spices? How India is the link between Persia and China in the spice trade? I know your uncle taught you about records and numbers in the keeping of his books.' Mrs Lal stopped and paused. She cupped my face in her hands and said, 'Arjun, open your heart, not only your eyes and ears. Then you will understand what you hold in your head.'

The note read, 'Paper and pen for your studies.'

***

I am sitting in the workshop with my bapuji; he has helped me these last few months, during his recovery, to design a doll. We named it Maroon Star Doll. It is a student dressed with a graduation gown and carrying books. The original Maroon Star Doll, with a real maroon star ruby at the neck of the gown, sits at his right hand. He is laughing, his excitement catching as our friends gather around.

'Look, look. Here you are, Mr Mangal.' He read. "Kings and royalty view the radiant red tones of the ruby as a symbol of strength, power, and wealth."

He is reading my words from 'Channapatna Dolls' by Arjun Basu.

Bapuji smiled at me. 'You and I will work together and be good friends', beta (*son*)?'

Music grew loud. The women started dancing, and the men cheered as I replied, 'So we will, baba, my father, so we will.'

Sandra Smiles

Previously published work.
Published in Scribblers Mandurah anthology 2020.

An Unexpected Encounter

Emmeline had arrived from her home in Australia to visit her cousins in the north of England. She had been planning this visit for a long time and had at last saved up enough money for her fare and to tide her over till she could find a job. She had quite an extended family throughout the country whom she had never met. She was a qualified nurse so thought she would have no trouble in finding employment, either in the hospital system or privately with an aged care agency. When this story takes place, she is staying with an elderly cousin, Ruby Illingworth, on the edge of a large town in the north of England. Housing estates are gradually taking over the countryside, but where Cousin Ruby lives, there is still unspoilt country within walking distance.

Cousin Ruby was quite a character; she was the same generation as Emmeline's mother but older. She lived up to her name, Ruby, by always wearing something red. She also owned several pieces of jewellery incorporating rubies, given to her over the years by her late husband. She was a keen gardener and grew prize-winning roses. There was still a good display of them in the garden, and Emmeline noticed they were mainly in shades of red which made her smile.

One afternoon while Cousin Ruby was at a meeting of the Women's Institute, Emmeline took herself off for a walk through the nearby woods. A derelict mansion stood hidden in the woods. The local people said it was haunted, but Emmeline rather dismissed the idea. Who really believes in ghosts these days? However, there was a certain atmosphere about this place. It had had an unsettled history long before the present day.

One of the coal barons back in the 1800s had built it. When his fortunes failed, it had stood empty for some time. During the time of the Great War of 1914-1918, the current owner of the abandoned property arranged for the building to be converted into a hospital for the wounded. The war ended and eventually authorities repatriated the last patients to convalescent homes. Then once again it was empty. By this time, it was showing its age for the owner had done little maintenance over the intervening years.

Mr and Mrs Williamson, an enterprising couple, bought it at an incredibly low price thinking they could turn it into a boarding school for young children whose parents worked overseas. They planned to make it into a holiday home as well, for such children who could not return to their parents in the holidays. They would also take in extra children in the same circumstances from other schools. This worked well for a few years. It was a lot of hard work even though they employed good staff. Finally, it was no longer making a profit. The Williamsons were beginning to look towards retirement, and the house again needed repairs. World news was not good with World War II about to begin.

The Williamsons put the house on the market. The local council needed a suitable place for the children evacuated from the orphanage in the nearby city. Officialdom thought they would be safer in the country rather than the city which the enemy would probably be targeting. Tucked away in the country as it was, it seemed a safe place. The Williamsons retired to live near their daughter in the south, and the staff from the city orphanage with the children moved in. Life continued for the house as before.

In the post-war era, ideas about caring for children changed and institutions like the orphanage ceased to exist as foster care was deemed more suitable for the children. Once again, the house stood empty. This time it stayed empty, gradually falling into disrepair and ruin. Squatters came and went. There had been ideas about turning it into a youth hostel, but nothing came of that. The costs would have been too great for the council to consider it.

From time to time, it seemed as though the ghosts of the past inhabited it. There were reports of lights sometimes seen. Gradually the gardens became overgrown as trees and shrubs grew and took over. A bad storm one winter knocked tiles from the roof. A branch crashed down, breaking a few windowpanes. The homeless squatters who came for shelter caused a fire one evening. They managed to extinguish it in good time, but more damage had occurred. Squatters never liked to stay there long. They said they could hear the cries of the wounded soldiers. Others maintained it was the cries of homesick children or the sad waif-like orphans.

There was a well-trodden path that led along the edge of the woods. The path Emmeline was following curved closer to the woods. It had been raining earlier, but with raincoat and muffler she was well protected. As Cousin Ruby said, "If you let a bit of rain stop you, you would never go anywhere!"

Emmeline noticed the track was following what seemed to be an overgrown stone wall. Nettles grew in profusion and rambling roses had rambled over the top of it. She wondered if there were a gate anywhere. She could not see a break in the cover but kept looking. At last, rewarded, she saw what looked like two gate posts standing out from the covering vegetation. As she neared them, she could see a broken wrought-iron gate leaning haphazardly, supported only by broken, rusted hinges. There was a good gap which she squeezed through and then followed what must have been the original driveway. Cousin Ruby had told her about the old mansion and had shown her a couple of pictures in a book about places of interest. The book, published a long time ago, showed pictures of people in Edwardian clothes. Emmeline was curious and wanted to see it for herself.

The house must have originally had extensive grounds when the coal baron had first had it built. He would have employed a large staff for both inside and outside. Perhaps he had been trying to buy his way into society by entertaining the local gentry with lavish parties and balls. Emmeline wondered about his family. Did his wife enjoy the move from a humbler existence, or was she overwhelmed by the change? Cousin Ruby had mentioned a daughter who had done well for herself, but she did not know anything more.

Emmeline could see stonework through the trees and realised she must have nearly reached the mansion. She was glad the drizzling rain had stopped as she shook the drops off her raincoat and removed her beret to shake it too. Fortunately, she had been wearing stout shoes, so her feet were still dry and warm in her thick socks. The house was gloomy under the leaden sky. She walked up the flight of broken stone steps. The chipped stone balustrade had some bits missing. A stone urn lay on its side. Someone had boarded up a few of the broken windows, but they did not seem very secure. It looked as though people had gained access to the house by pulling off some of the boards. She tried the front door unsuccessfully, but it was firmly shut, either locked or so warped by the weather it would not move. She peered through one of the windows but could see nothing of interest, just bits of rubbish on the floor.

Emmeline decided to walk around the building before trying to get in and so followed a narrow path round to the side. There would have been more lawns here, but it was difficult to put it into perspective. Several decades of children using the grounds for playing fields would not have done the lawns any good. At the back of the house seemed to be the remains of an orchard with a curved brick wall. This would probably have been where the gardener had fruit trees espaliered against the wall to catch the sunlight and to hold the warmth. There was little to show now.

Emmeline continued past old potting sheds. She looked through the broken doorways seeing flowerpots and rusty implements. In one, there were slatted shelves for storage of fruit or for setting herbs to dry. Emmeline remembered her mother cutting lavender to dry. Eventually, she arrived at what was probably the kitchen door. She found it unlocked and gave it a push. It opened easily, and she thought someone must have been used it recently.

She stepped inside. Tiny claws of fear ran up her spine and across her scalp. What was she doing here? All the horror, murder and mystery movies she had watched on television overtook her mind. Still, she pressed on through the scullery and small storeroom to the kitchen with its great iron range. Someone *had* obviously been here recently. A faint smell of food lingered, but there was no heat in the stove when she touched it. Little light came through the dirty windows, but there was enough for her to see her way into the main part of the building. There seemed to be a warren of small rooms in this 'below-stairs' section. In its heyday, it must have been a real baronial hall.

Through to the main part, there were enormous reception rooms and a banqueting hall. The staircase leading to the next floor branched halfway with stairs going left and right turning back on themselves to the landing and passages on either side. It did not look safe with broken banisters and some steps also broken. Someone had put a barricade across, but it looked as though people had managed to get past it.

It was an eerie place, and she thought it no wonder there were so many stories told about it. The locked bedroom and the mad wife; that was a bit too much like a Bronte story. Perhaps orphans locked up for punishment and forgotten for a day or two. Were the children who spent both their school days and the holidays here happy? It could be a lovely place, but even so, the wind across the moors would be a mournful sound if you were unhappy. The winters too would have been cold – chilblains on toes and fingers.

Emmeline's granny, Frances, had said if it had not been for the second world war, her parents might have left her in such a place. Fortunately for her, the war had started before her parents had made any definite plans. She had been able to stay with her parents and attend at service-run schools overseas until the end of the war. When her father finally retired, they eventually made their home in Australia, and Frances had finished her education there.

Emmeline, who had always lived at home, wondered what it would be like left in such a place. Nowadays air travel shortened the time spent travelling so it was possible for children in similar circumstances to see their parents more frequently. She thought it must be terrible to be stuck in a place like this for a whole year or more with only letters to keep you in touch. Even with letters, the surface mail would take time.

The venture to England to meet her extended family was really the first time she had travelled so far away. To her, it was a real adventure. This so-called haunted house was also a challenge and something new. Then a crash from above made her jump. Was it something that had fallen or was someone up there? She had been aware of various creaks and noises but had decided that, as it was an old house, one would expect odd noises. Then she thought she heard a moan. Surely there could not be someone up there should she venture up the stairs to see if there were?

Emmeline listened carefully. There *was* something up there. Carefully and quietly, she eased her way past the barrier and, testing each stair-tread, went up slowly. Should she turn left or right when she reached the dividing point? She was on the left-hand side so took the left branch. The two sections ended on a landing with corridors going in both directions.

She called out. "Is anyone there?"

There seemed to be a shuffling sound and again what she thought was a moan or low groan. It sounded as though it was coming from further down the left-hand corridor. Emmeline went cautiously in that direction. The light coming through the windows over the stairwell was gloomy from the dirt on them, but there was sufficient for her to see her way.

Though the closed doors along the corridor kept it dark, she could see some light coming through the last doorway, which showed her it must be open. She continued along and cautiously peered around the door. At first, there seemed to be nothing there except some old bits of furniture stacked against the wall and a heap of what looked like some carpets or mats in one corner. For the second time, she asked, "Is anyone there?" Then, "Can I help you?"

"Oh! yes please," a voice croaked. "I fell and hit my head, and I think I may have broken something."

"Who are you, and what are you doing here?" asked Emmeline as she came into the room. She could see someone on the floor partly propped up by an old wooden chest.

"I work for the local real estate company. My boss asked me to look the place over and make a report. It seems someone is at last interested in the property. I came upstairs to look through the rooms. While trying to move the shutter on that window, I slipped and fell. I hit my head. I feel a bit funny. I did try my mobile, but it must be out of range, and the battery is low. My ankle is very painful, and I can't put any weight on it. Do you think you could help me or else get some help?"

Emmeline approached him. "I'll see what I can do. It might be just a sprain, but with a head injury, you should see a doctor. My mobile is not working either. With my help, do you think you could stand? I am Emmeline. What's your name?"

"Timothy," he said, "or most people call me Tim.".

"I am usually Emma, or Emmy. I'll tear a strip of this curtain lining." She indicated a small heap of curtains in the corner. 'Then if I bind your ankle firmly, you may have enough support with me helping you to get you downstairs."

There were some bits of wood lying in a heap from a broken chest of drawers and bedside table. One of the table legs was a good stout piece about the right length. She went over to Tim. She bound his ankle firmly, having decided it was probably just a sprain and not broken. Then between them, he managed to stand on one leg and with her support and the piece of wood, they managed to reach the top of the stairs. Emmeline helped Tim down on the first two steps. Then suggested he should sit on top step and, still sitting, work himself down step by step till he reached the last ones when she could help up him again.

"How did you get here?" she asked. "Do you have a car?"

"I left it parked on the roadside and walked to the entrance. I had found the gates impossible to open so left it and came in. I did not think I would be here long. I am glad you came when you did. I don't know what I would have done."

"It is quite a hike to the gates. Do you think you could manage as we have done so far? I could go and get help but that would mean leaving you here for some time. I think we had better try to get you to the car. Have some water before we start. You don't want to get dehydrated." She handed him her water bottle.

They made their way slowly down to the gate. Eventually, after having frequent stops on the way and squeezing through the gates, they followed the path to the road.

'The car is still there and hasn't been vandalised or towed away. I am surprised I didn't see it when I arrived. But then I came from a different direction and was not expecting to see any vehicles parked near the place." Said Emmeline, "Is it manual or automatic? I don't have a driver's license for over here yet, otherwise I could drive you. If it is automatic, you could probably manage as it was your left foot you injured. Would you like me to come with you anyway? I am living with my cousin, but she is out for the afternoon and won't be back for ages otherwise, she could take you to the Medical Centre."

"I think I will be all right now," said Tim. "Thank you for your help. That bandage is good. The car is automatic, and as you say, my left foot is the one I injured. It feels much better even though we had to take that long walk."

"I think we are probably still out of range here, but could you let me have your number for when your mobile is working again?" asked Emmeline. "I would like to know how you got on."

"Yes, here's my card" Tim held one out to her. "Would you give me your Cousin Ruby's telephone number or your mobile one for when you are in range?" He scribbled the numbers down as she spoke. Emmeline helped Tim into the car. Once sitting on the driver's seat, he seemed to recover.

"This is better. I will get round to the Medical Centre for a check-up and let you know the verdict. Thank you so much. I don't know how I could have coped if you had not turned up. We must meet up again before you continue your travels. Bye for now." With that, he took off slowly, giving her a wave as he left.

Well! How was that for an unexpected adventure? Emmeline said to herself. I hope he keeps in touch. We did not get around to exchanging personal details, and he probably has a steady girlfriend or fiancée. It is no good getting too involved with anyone. I will be moving on soon – back down to London where I have a temporary job waiting for me and other rellies to meet.

Alison P. Smith.

Retribution

"Is it OK if I take the last of the smoked salmon for my sandwiches this morning, dear?" Baxter called out to Sheila, his wife. "I don't want to go to the canteen. It seems a pity to waste it if you don't want it for yourself."

"Take what you want." his wife replied. "I am going out for lunch today, if you remember."

They had had a dinner party on the Saturday evening for some friends, John and Betty Murray, who had come up from their country town in the south. They were celebrating their Ruby Wedding by having a short holiday in the city and catching up with old friends. Sheila enjoyed putting on dinner parties and this was a good excuse. They had invited two other couples known to the visitors and it had been a great evening. Baxter smiled in remembrance. Smoked salmon had been on the menu as part of the entrée, and to celebrate, they had opened the two bottles of Sparkling Red the Murrays had brought from their local winery. It seemed a fitting wine for a Ruby Wedding celebration.

Baxter made up two rounds of sandwiches using slices of homemade bread and cut the sandwiches in half diagonally. He thought the smoked salmon needed more respect than a simple cheese and ham sandwich. He would have cut those straight across. With some home-grown baby spinach, he put the sandwiches into a chilled pouch he took from the fridge. He then packed up his briefcase and set off for the station. He had at least an hour's train journey before reaching the CBD where his office was situated.

On arrival in the city, Baxter quickly walked the three blocks to one of the tall buildings. His office was on the seventh floor there. The day was already becoming hotter. He caught the lift and said "Good morning" to his fellow workers while waiting to reach his floor.

The small kitchen and dining area near the offices was well set up. He took his sandwiches out of the chilled pouch and put them in the fridge. He was thankful for the pouch as it had already lost most of its coldness during the long journey to the office. His sandwiches still seemed cold enough.

It had been a busy morning and Baxter had been in a conference which took up most of it. There had been no time for a morning break with coffee and a bite to eat. By one o'clock, he was looking forward to his smoked salmon sandwiches.

Baxter returned to his own floor and entered the little kitchen where he made himself some coffee and went to retrieve the sandwiches.

"Who has been eating my lunch?" he asked himself. Two sandwiches had gone and when he looked, he saw a bite had been taken out one of the remaining two. In disgust, he dropped them in the bin and, after drinking his coffee, headed for the canteen. He had to join the queue and there was not much choice left. He felt understandably annoyed. It was grossly unfair, and besides, it was stealing. Surely, we were all paid enough, he thought, so it was not necessary to take someone else's food. Perhaps the lunch just looked too tempting.

Baxter went back to the office somewhat disgruntled after an unsatisfactory canteen lunch. He looked around the office.

"Where is Godfrey?" he asked, noting the empty cubicle.

"Oh, he went to the First Aid post or rather he was taken there. He was suffering terrible stomach pains and was violently sick," someone replied.

"We think it might have been food poisoning," said another.

"He muttered something about fish sandwiches."

"Oh! Did he now?" said Baxter.

He smiled to himself and thought, I have found the lunch thief. It serves him right if he is sick.

It was perhaps just as well he had not eaten his own lunch after all. Sheila had bought the smoked salmon on Friday afternoon, and it was now Monday. What with one thing and another, he thought the salmon might have gone off, though it had seemed all right when he made his sandwiches that morning. He hoped Godfrey had learnt his lesson and would be more circumspect about helping himself to other people's food now.

Alison P. Smith

The Second Ruby

Ruby … 'rare precious stone' according to the dictionary.

I have had two Rubys in my life, but neither was a rare and precious stone.

The first was the deputy headmistress of the high school where I completed the Junior Certificate in the 1940s. Can you imagine my surprise on my wedding day as I entered the Church, I saw not only my first Ruby, but also the headmistress of the school, sitting in the back row! They had come to see me – an ex-student – married! Maybe the fact that I had been Head Girl in my last year at school was the reason for their presence.

My other Ruby was a dear friend. I met her when my husband spent respite time in Spencer Lodge Nursing Home in Albany. Ruby's husband was a resident. Both men were battling Alzheimers. Ruby visited Martin every day to assist him with his meal. With both our men facing the same problem, we soon became friends. Our friendship continued after the death of our husbands.

Ruby's childhood was spent on the family farm. In her early teens, she was taken out of school to stay home to assist on the farm. Times were hard and this often happened in those early days. She later married Martin and farmed with him as they raised their sons. For some time after his death, Ruby was a lost soul.

My friend was a dear lady with a big heart who would do anything for anybody. She was delightfully uncomplicated and asked nothing more than to be a friend. For many years she worked voluntarily in the little shop in the hospital and also took on the job of arranging the flowers that were brought in for patients. She had many friends and was always pleased to find ways to help them.

She was a talented China painter and a valued member of the local group. She also wrote poetry and was persuaded to join our Writers Circle. At each meeting, we enjoyed her varied selection, and they were a welcome addition to the books we produced. I have to say that she didn't READ her work … she could recite every one of the pieces she composed. She endeared herself to us all with her insight into both rural life, as well as the highlights of Albany, both of which featured in her poetry. Ruby loved the city of Albany with a passion. She really enjoyed the social side of our group and made us laugh with her jokes.

When Ruby said with a twinkle in her eye and a cheeky smile, "Did you hear about …" we knew we were in for a chuckle!

This delightful lady also had another skill. She could produce music at the drop of a hat from her harmonica, which she kept in her bag at all times. As one member of the group said, "At Christmas time, birthday celebrations, or even just because she felt like it, she would pluck her well-worn harmonica from her handbag and give a short rendition of *Click go the Shears* or some other jaunty tune."

Sadly, Alzheimers began to take its toll on our dear friend, and we were concerned because she was likely to lose her way when she drove to meetings. We fixed this problem gently by delegating a member to pick her up. A special bond grew between these two ladies, which was a joy to witness. Despite her problems with Alzheimers, Ruby could still remember her poems.

She died at the age of 92 years. Her friend and mentor from the Writers Group said at her funeral,

"Ruby was a treasured member of our Writers Group and we will miss her wonderful poetry, her shy smile and the twinkle in her eye. Thank you, Ruby, for your kind and loving heart."

On second thoughts, the dictionary's description wasn't far wrong.

Molly Smith

Ruby Relocates

It's love at first sight, but her head is clear enough to ensure the heart doesn't dominate Ruby's thoughts before making the final decision. All the relevant paperwork is prepared and signed.

But now, Ruby has many emotions swirling as the SOLD sticker is pressed across the For Sale sign. For the last ten years, she's called this place home, but it's been snapped up quickly in the current real estate frenzy. Two weeks ago, while on holiday down south, she'd stumbled across a neglected dwelling tucked away in a small quiet rural community. Ruby had driven past it many times before venturing inside, again and again that week.

Her friends and family cannot understand how a young single woman in her mid-thirties feels compelled to move so far away from them. Their comments never stop:

"Who's going to help you fix that old dump up?"

"It's freezing cold down there."

"It costs more to live in the country."

"You won't know anyone."

Her usual responses are like a broken record:

"I always enjoy my visits down south."

"I'm moving to a peaceful community."

"I love the new home I'm moving to."

Eventually, Ruby selectively chooses not to listen anymore.

Moving from a large abode into a much smaller one finds her anguishing over what to keep and what to sell online. This requires Ruby to honestly evaluate what items are important and WHAT will fit into her new home. At times Ruby finds it difficult, but is motivated by looking at the new photos on her phone. These give her the spark she needs to keep going.

Moving day approaches like a jet plane landing at the airport; all of a sudden it is time for the wheels to hit the tarmac. Emotions wibble and wobble all over the place too.

Ruby witnesses a spectacular sunrise and sees this as a positive omen. The removalists swing into action and soon everything is in the back of the truck.

Four hours later, Ruby has the keys and is opening the front door in her new neighbourhood. But where is the truck, she wonders?

Hours later, the fully laden truck finally appears.

"Did you stop at the Tavern to have a counter meal?" Ruby queries as the driver opens his door.

He lands on the driveway with a thud. His face looks like a thunderstorm.

Oops, in a split-second Ruby realises that was the wrong thing to say. This guy is not happy!

He stomps menacingly towards Ruby. Angry words explode in her direction, like they're being ejected from an erupting volcano.

"YOUR place does NOT exist on Google. We've been going up and down for hours looking for you. Eventually, we asked for help from an old fella. He looked us up and down, then started having a coughing fit. I thought he was going to keel right over in front of us. And blow me down, then he takes his time to roll another cigarette and dangles it from his gob. He looked me straight in the eye and with a cheeky chuckle said 'What's the rush? Sun's still up. It's country o'clock here, mate! So, I shouted back at him, Bl…… H…., if I operated like that back in the city, no work would ever get done."

The agitated removalist is now shouting louder and louder by the second, while at the same time ripping doors open so the truck can finally be unloaded.

"Well, I can tell you, Missy, that is NOT what I wanted to hear. I promised my missus I'd be home in time to celebrate our 25th wedding anniversary at a fancy restaurant tonight. Even you will hear the explosion later on tonight."

Briefly, the truck driver stops to gather his breath before resuming his rant.

"The old bloke finally told us he knows the history to this area and for us to drive exactly five kilometres out of town. Then turn right onto the gravel road, that's locally known as the Road to Nowhere. Apparently, years ago someone pinched the sign as a souvenir. Ha, your town's nicknamed Nowhere! Then he cautioned me to keep my eyes peeled or we'd never find you! Well, we knew that part anyway."

He glares at Ruby. "Now show me where I can shove all this stuff".

A belly laugh is desperately wanting to escape. Ruby battles to control it, but she hides it with a smile. "Yes, of course. This way please. I'd love to make you a cup of tea, but the kettle and the tea bags are buried in one of those boxes."

Furniture and boxes are thrown haphazardly all over the place, rapidly filling up the small space within her home. The rest is dumped higgledy-piggledy in the small garage.

Ruby groans. "Oh no, I think I still have too much stuff. I'm not sure if there's even any space left for me to walk around in here. How am I going to find anything? And there's no room left in the garage for my car."

Basic items for the kitchen, bathroom and bedroom are found and placed accordingly. She'll wait until tomorrow to open any more boxes.

After making the bed and having a shower, she settles in her favourite rocker recliner. But as Ruby begins sipping on a freshly brewed pot of tea, there's a knock at the door.

"Oh, no!" Ruby sighs as she wearily trudges to the door.

Two beaming faces peer in at her. Hands are thrust forward, as a voice says, "Here's a casserole to help you settle in on your first night."

Instantly, Ruby feels her body relax as a delicious aroma escapes from the casserole dish.

The tall woman looks down at Ruby and quietly says, "Welcome to our town. My name's Hilda, but everyone calls me Helpful Hilda. My husband's known as Kind Kevin. And so you hear it from us, we have a marriage made in heaven!"

"Yes," continues Kevin. "If there's anything we can do, please ask. We live across the road at number six.

Their words are like a steam train; they just keep coming.

Eventually, Ruby is able to say, "Thanks. I'm Ruby, but don't have a nickname!"

Kevin interrupts with a mischievous grin, "Don't worry, Ruby, you'll have one soon."

Ruby's eyes twinkle. "We'll wait and see about that, won't we?"

Briefly, she pauses but doesn't allow him anytime to respond.

"I'm exhausted. It's been a very long day, so I appreciate you've made my tea."

As Ruby returns to the lounge room, she gazes at the fireplace. No fire has been lit in it for many years. She knows it's essential to have a fully functioning fireplace.

Pulling out a notepad. she writes: LIST :* Chimney Sweep * Firewood * Kindling * Matches.

Ruby decides to use her portable electric room heater and a spare blanket to keep herself warm. It appears the evening chill begins to seep into this old home during mid-afternoon.

Rain begins to fall as Ruby snuggles up in bed. She is mesmerized by the sound of rain on the corrugated rooftop. It weaves its magic, coaxing her to fall asleep with ease.

During the night, Ruby shivers as she makes her way by

torchlight to the toilet, located on the back verandah. Wooden floorboards creak and groan while doors squeak on their hinges. Mentally, she adds more to the list she started earlier in the day.

With bedroom curtains open, Ruby springs out of bed as the first rays of daylight filter in. With not a minute to lose, she quickly dresses and exits her home to investigate her new neighbourhood.

She discovers there's a mixture of both old and new homes; all are in varying stages of care. Some have manicured gardens, and others are full of weeds. There's a whiff of smoke from wood fires keeping each residence warm overnight. The sun warms her back. The earlier chorus of birdsong is quietening down.

Back home, Ruby eyeballs the rusty front gate that's permanently propped open. Moving her gaze to the picket fence, she notices many pickets are missing. Weeds seem to have a mind of their own! Many have crawled up, over, through and under whatever obstacle is in their way to escape the confines of the property. They are venturing onto the footpath, into the roadside gutter and invading the neighbours' yards. Strolling towards the front door, Ruby glances at the weatherboard planking. A shabby grey smudge colour sadly beckons for her to restore it back to its original vibrant blue.

Ruby picks up her notepad and adds to the list she started yesterday: * Spray lubricant for the door hinges * Warm floor mats * Quotes from contractors for fencing options * Gardener and Landscaper * Painter * WINTER DRESSING GOWN!

Ruby's cottage is old, but it has character. Someone a long time ago gave it the love it deserved. Now it's her turn to lavish her new home with tender loving care. She has adequate money to renovate, rejuvenate and replenish it. Ruby knows even though there will be many obstacles, there will also be solutions.

A knock at the door startles Ruby.

"Hello," Ruby says to a woman of similar height, but who fills the width of the door.

"G'day. My name's Mumma Megan. Welcome to town. Come over for a cuppa and freshly baked scones."

"Thank you. I will."

Conversation flows easily between them. She discovers Megan's husband is nicknamed Happy Henry. He returns back to the table when more food appears or another hot drink is on offer.

While sipping on their third, or was it their fourth pot of tea, Megan continues. "Watch out for Nosey Nicole as she will want to know everything about your past and what your future plans are. And then there's Cranky Carolyn, Grumpy Gwen and Irritable Irene. Accept them just as they are and don't be offended by anything they say. Loud Larry is married to Quiet Quincie and they are a loving couple who will help you in any way. Fussy Frank and Difficult Dan have a few issues, so be cautious around them. However, before you know it, they'll let you enter into their lives. Harry and I have been together since we met as childhood sweethearts. We love each other to bits. Any time you feel down in the dumps, come over and I'll brighten up your day".

Mumma Megan pauses momentarily to catch her breath.

"Overall, we're a small tight-knit community. We love being off the beaten track. If we want noise, we drive thirty minutes towards the coast and it's always there waiting for us!"

"I've only been here for one day and I'm sure very soon I too will be moving at a snail's pace," Ruby responds.

Later she opens her computer to send a short message to friends and family. She advises them she's settling in and has already met some of her neighbours.

Ruby pauses to glance around her home. The reality of the task at hand hits her full force. There is a lot of work to be done.

Quickly she catches her thoughts and puts the brakes on them.

'No,' she thinks, 'I'm not giving anyone the satisfaction of saying 'We told you so!' After all, I've only been here one day.'

Looking back at her cheery email, she finishes it off by sending everyone her love. Quickly, she returns to the top of the email and in the subject line writes Ruby Relocates.

Maxine Spencer

The R and R Residence

Stormy weather is descending upon the city. Large ominous, gloomy clouds of many shades of grey threaten to dump a dam full of rain on anything and everyone in its path. Many layers of clothing, along with umbrellas at the ready on the back seat, is all they require.

Every Sunday, Christopher and Melanie drive to an unknown destination, taking turns to sit behind the steering wheel. This all began four years ago, on their first date. Since then, they have zig-zagged all over the place, from the ocean to the hills and either side of the Swan River. They've discovered many places others never knew existed. Parks of all sorts, a variety of shopping centres, a myriad of entertainment precincts, walking trails of all descriptions and eateries aplenty have appeared before them in all directions on the compass. Even though they are always on the lookout for their future dream home, they realise purchasing one will be sometime in the distant future.

While waiting at the traffic lights only five minutes from home, Christopher glances to his right. Through the driver's window, a rainbow is beginning to form in the distance, south of Perth.

He mentally calculates, at the next set of lights he will alter the direction he's driving in.

With eyebrows arched and wearing a big grin, Christopher blurts out, "Hey, Melanie, today's a great day to find out if there's really a pot of gold at the end of a rainbow."

As quick as a wink and with a sparkle in her eyes, she turns to look at her husband. "And you know how much I love treasure hunts."

Pausing momentarily, she allows her thoughts to swirl. As they bubble to the surface, words form with ease. "Do you know what? I've just had an idea! We've been going on these Mystery Drives ever since we met. So, I'm going to start writing about them. I reckon I can fill a book very quickly."

"Ahh, what a great idea. But you don't like writing. You hated English at school."

"You're right. I hated it with a vengeance. But that was when I was at school. I'm a big girl now and no one's telling me to write topics that are in the curriculum anymore. This *is* something I want to do. I'm going to give it a go, starting from today!"

The young couple drive past many suburbs and industrial areas until finally they reach the southern seaside holiday destination of Rockingham, where they figure the rainbow has beckoned them to visit. Even though it has now disappeared, it's been replaced by many colours flashing on the OPEN sign at the entrance of a small café. This is nestled in amongst other buildings looking out over the beach.

Once seated, they order and eat a scrumptious lunch while guessing what surprises they're going to discover in this new location. As they leave the café, they turn left to investigate the street further. They immediately view a selection of properties for sale next door in the Real Estate Agency's window. Their eyes drift over the wide choice available, until one piques Melanie's attention.

Urgent Sale. Price Reduced. Owners required to relocate immediately. Enquire within for more details.

Grabbing Christopher's arm, she pulls him inside before he has a chance to say anything.

Melanie looks at the salesman and, with words tumbling out of her mouth at a rapid rate, she splutters,

"Iwanttoknowmoreaboutthathousewithapricereductionthatis anurgentsale?"

With a smile erupting, the salesman puts his hands up in disbelief. "Hang on a minute. Stop. I have no idea what you just said. By the way, my name is Daniel. Now tell me what's in the window that has got you so excited. But first, take a deep breath and slow down before you say it again!"

Melanie and Christopher look each other and burst out laughing.

"Sorry, Daniel. She's got a habit of doing that. My name's Christopher and this is my wife, Melanie."

Melanie composes herself and, at a slower pace, says, "I want to know more about the house with an urgent sale and has a price reduction."

"Ahh, yes. That one's a bargain. Come on, jump in my car and we'll go and have a look at it."

While driving slowly near Rockingham's beachfront, the coastline continues into the next suburb of Safety Bay. Daniel highlights all the advantages of living in this peaceful seaside community.

"And here is the home you were asking about, Melanie," says Daniel as he drives up a sandy driveway onto the property.

Melanie's heart sinks as she looks at a front yard covered with many pigface plants. The only thing she likes is the masses of hot pink daisy-like flowers that greet her.

She looks further afield. There are no fences. Mentally she puts another big cross against the house, as it offers no privacy.

"Hang on, where are all the neighbours?" mumbles Melanie.

Daniel is quick to reply. "Warnbro is a new suburb, with people gradually buying the land to build their dream home. It won't be long, and this will be a bustling and thriving place to live in. You have the chance to develop what has already been started."

He gives them only a moment before continuing. "Now come on, let's go inside."

Reluctantly, the young couple awkwardly step out of the car and slowly trudge towards the home that is no longer tugging at Melanie's heartstrings.

As Melanie walks through the front door, she moans. "Oh no! No carpet and no curtains. Oh dear, what else am I going to find?"

A bright orange benchtop greets them in the kitchen. "Oh, at last something I do like. I adore the colour orange." These words slip unexpectantly from between Melanie's lips before she has time to clamp her mouth shut. She no longer wants to show any interest in this house. So, why did those words slip out so quickly? she wonders silently.

The bathroom is also adorned in bright orange. When she pushes open the next door, the toilet sits proudly with an orange cistern and seat. Melanie can't help the long chuckle that bursts forth. "Oh, no! Thank goodness I love the colour orange. It's in here too, Christopher," she groans while calling out to her husband.

The salesman is keen to make a sale today. He immediately uses the colour orange to his advantage.

"This home is only two years old, and has lots of potential. It's a spacious four-bedroom home that the owners have not had the funds to completely furnish or establish yet. So, that makes THIS an ideal property for YOU to purchase. It gives you the power to make all the decisions on what happens next. And remember, you are only five minutes from the local beach to go swimming all year round."

Briefly, he pauses to allow the information to settle.

"I've had immense interest in this home based on the price, so you will need to make a quick decision to secure it as yours".

Until now, Christopher has kept his thoughts to himself.

"Daniel, can you step outside for a moment, so we can discuss our options, please?"

"Of course I can. Take all the time you need," Daniel replies as he wanders back out to where his car is parked.

Holding Melanie's hand, Christopher gently guides her around the house. As they walk, he begins to express himself.

"Melanie, this house IS a bargain. We have a deposit saved; one that will secure a home of our own, providing it is THIS house. I actually love this home and the coastal community is a bonus. Anything you don't like, we can modify or change as required, including the curtains, floor coverings, fencing and gardens. By buying this place, we'll be able to leave the rat race behind; a place where we will never be able to afford to buy our own home anytime soon."

He gives Melanie time to consider everything, then waits patiently for her to respond in her own time.

They are both standing in silence, pondering all the possibilities. When Daniel suddenly bursts through the door.

"Sorry to intrude, but I've just received a phone call. Another interested party is ready to sign on the dotted line and purchase this home. So, I must have your decision immediately."

Melanie and Christopher glance at each other, nod and in unison exclaim, "It's Sold!"

Back at the office, all the relevant paperwork is completed and signatures seal the deal. Everyone shakes hands and the young couple are congratulated.

Stepping back out onto the footpath, Christopher and Melanie decide to continue investigating what else is nearby. They amble along until Melanie catches sight of a Jeweler's shop. As usual, Melanie takes the lead and ventures inside.

Soon she spots one ring of many colours."What is that?" she asks the sales assistant.

"That's an Opal. It's like looking at a rainbow, isn't it?"

Instantly Melanie and Christopher look at each other, gasp and once again, in unison say , "It's Sold."

Then Melanie spots another ring in the next cabinet. Within moments, both the opal and ruby rings perch on her fingers. She moves each hand from side to side. Both rings pull at Melanie's heartstrings. The minutes tick by, and she finds it difficult to decide which one to purchase. With a sigh, Christopher quietly suggests she buy both!

Her face lights up. "Really, are you sure? We can't afford to get both."

"It's not every day we buy our own home. You deserve both rings, Melanie."

As they drive home, Melanie holds the signed Contract of Sale paperwork on her lap. At the same time, she's unable to take her eyes off the two sparkling rings that now snugly fit on each finger.

Thinking out loud, Melanie continues. "Well, today's mystery drive is one I will never forget because we did find lots of treasure at the end of the rainbow. I'm going to arrange for a personalized wooden house sign to be designed and crafted. It will hang proudly on the verandah near the front door. We can call our new home Rainbow, Ruby or Opal. Which one do you like best?"

Christopher chuckles. "Oh no, that's not my decision. You're in charge of that!"

Melanie juggles the three options around in her mind, carefully considering each one in turn.

Moments before getting back to their rental in suburbia, Melanie turns towards Christopher. "Ok, I've finally made a decision. I would like to officially call our new home 'The R and R Residence'."

With a puzzled expression, Christopher looks at his wife as he queries, "As in Rest and Relaxation?"

She bursts out laughing. "No! But that's exactly what I want everyone to say. I'm going to have lots of fun revealing how a mystery drive, a rainbow and a ring, or two, lured us to a community where we purchased our own home. I look forward to welcoming everyone to 'The Rainbow and Ruby Residence'."

Maxine Spencer

Ruby's Tuesday

Acknowledging Mick Jagger and Keith Richards for title, slightly tweaked.

Ruby's eyes widened as she stared through the rain-washed window at the vision before her. Silhouetted against a sapphire blue sky, the verge of trees dazzled, each leaf polished and buffed, free of dust brought in by the wind of the last few days. On the horizon, but not yet to fullness, a golden orb seeped sunbeams into the room to form a river full and flowing with gold, ruby red, and silver sparkles. It filled the area before capturing her in a cocoon. A river of enchantment. 'Good morning, magical day,' she breathed. Hesitant to break the moment, a glance at the clock told her she should leave to avoid being late for work.

Outside her door, rays and streams of dust drifted over homes and cars, creating a spell-binding picture. A gossamer cloud of sparkles settled on her, bringing calmness, and for the first time in weeks she looked forward to this Tuesday school day.

Tuesdays – not the beginning of the week, not the end of the week, nor the peak of the week, that was Wednesday; no Ruby considered Tuesday's ordinary.

But today was different. The morning's tranquillity stayed with her until she approached the turnoff into school. Colleagues' voices resonated in her mind, conversations about the principal's wife. Standard talk over the past few weeks. Her illness had overshadowed the once genial staff. Conversations that continued as she walked through the corridors.

‘How do you think Greg will be today?’

‘Don’t know. Poor bloke. Gotta feel sorry for him.’

‘Yeah, hard, though. Sometimes when I need to talk to him, I don’t, he’s got enough worries.’

‘He and Jan get the results of her chemo soon, don’t they?’

‘I think today.’

And so, on went the talk.

Everybody respected Greg, but his manner had changed; his slumped shoulders and creased face showed his concern with his wife’s illness. The once enthusiastic school staff became sombre, reflecting Greg’s low spirits.

The gloomy conversations followed her to the classroom yet, still wrapped in her sparkles cocoon, Ruby smiled and nodded a greeting to everyone, 'Morning. Lovely day, isn't it?' to which each person lifted their eyebrows to question her comment.

Inside her room, she organised the usual English, spelling, and math lessons she had planned for the next few hours. Once the children arrived, the room would fill with bodies, and echo with the chatter of students and parents wishing to talk with her. Her usual day had begun.

As the class filled, through the mingle of voices, a barrage of thoughts again pounded in her mind, sentences, and phrases. She recalled past comments about someone not having had breakfast, about lost jobs and little money. Thoughts about doing other things rather than English, spelling, math; some wanted to paint, some to play outside, to build Lego, and other activities.

One thought filtered into Ruby’s mind: they lacked enthusiasm. She decided to make her special day into a day the children would remember. She glanced over her students before her eyes settled on Robbie, his creased clothes and too big sneakers. 'Robbie, come here.' The boy's shoulders drooped; he pouted as he slouched towards her, expecting trouble.

‘Have you had breakfast?’

'No.'

'Here's something for you.' Ruby opened her bag, took out a packet of cheese and crackers, and a banana.

'Take these to the corner and when you've finished, come to your desk.'

Robbie scuttled away, clutching the food. Ruby smiled, knowing a full stomach meant a happy child.

Problems like Robbie's were easy to solve; Ruby usually kept an amount of food for hungry children. Other problems were different. She could not solve out-of-school issues, but awareness meant better insight into her students.

Calling the class to order, she said, 'Today, we are going to have a special day.'

Twenty-five pairs of eyes looked at her; twenty-five voices all talked at once. 'What are we going to do, Miss?'

'Today is going to be your day; you can organise or change the lessons into what you would like to do.'

'Here's some paper. I want you to write down one project. Don't show anybody else, then we'll see what we've got.'

Ruby strolled among the desks, picked up each paper. After sorting, she announced, 'These are some activities you have written: play outside; weed the vegetable patch; read; write stories; have lunch near the native garden; and play on the adventure playground without children from other classes.'

The children talked at once. 'I want to …' echoed around the room until one child asked, 'Can we do some of those things?'

'We can do all of them.'

Ruby, still feeling the glow from her morning, wanted to enfold her charges into the bubble with which she began her day.

'We are going to have a happy day. This morning when I woke up, everything looked different; the garden was shining, and sunbeams sparkled through the window into my room. I felt happy, so I decided we would have a great day at school. We will have fun.'

'Wow!'

'That's good!' Exclamations echoed around the room.

'Let's get organised. We have thirty minutes to set the class up for your activities. Form yourselves into groups and get busy.'

Amidst the chaos, a knock came at the door, and Greg entered.

'What's going on in here?' Today, besides the frown that now seemed embedded on his forehead, the coldness in his voice chilled her. He looked around at the children – some moving tables and chairs, some setting out games, others making a corner for art, placing paper, shirts, brushes, and paint on a table.

'We're changing our day. The children are organising what they want to do.'

His frown deepened. 'What learning will they get out of that?'

'Look at them, they are showing a great deal of maturity at organising themselves and their activities, they are co-operating. They are having fun.'

He glanced around at the noisy, chaotic room, taking in the teamwork, the enthusiasm, the contentment. The frown remained, but the coldness in his voice mellowed to intrigue. 'I'm surprised. They are working and interacting well. I'll be interested to see how the day has gone later this afternoon.'

As he was leaving, Greg remarked, 'Your room feels different today. It is full of sunshine. Other classes are in shadow, but the sun has brightened and warmed your room.'

'Yes,' was all Ruby said.

Throughout the day, groups of children moved from activity to activity, recess extended beyond the bell. The children ate lunch in the school grounds near the garden, away from the hustle and bustle of the noisy and busy playground.

All the while, Greg watched, and as the day progressed, the hint of a smile hovered around his mouth.

Towards the end of the afternoon, her twenty-five charges sat on the floor around her chair.

Again, twenty-five voices babbled, this time about what a wonderful day it had been. As one voice, the class thanked her, said it was the best day they had ever had at school.

Ruby felt a warm glow inside herself. For each child, today had been a day to remember.

Before she left, Greg again entered her room. This time, a grin creased his face.

'Well done, Ruby. I am pleased with what you have achieved. This is what teaching is all about, children engaged, cooperating, working in teams … I could go on and on, but the faces of your students tell me you have had a successful day.'

'Thank you.' Her old Principal had returned, a man focused on having a well-run school. Ruby wanted to ask if he had heard about his wife's results; but would not unless Greg first said something. He stood straighter; the crease marks had lessened. Ruby felt his relief.

She wanted to wish him and Jan well, but said, 'It has been a precious day for the students and myself.'

'Yes, for me too,' Greg replied.

Ruby picked up her bag and walked to her car, thinking her Tuesday had been a perfect day.

Along the way, she noticed that, although her car still gleamed, the vibrancy was less vivid compared to this morning. The cacophony of thoughts from earlier in the day had ceased, and the river of glints and glistens had dispersed. She hoped the red, gold and silver glitter river, which that morning flowed to her from the golden orb, had now drifted to another person to also give them a gem of a day.

Lorraine Spring

Ruby and Silver

Hidden behind a rocky outcrop, Ruby scanned the plains and watched as the last stragglers stumbled up the gangplank. Despite Silver's urging, she could not look away, much less leave, until the last of them completed their journey. Some had flown there, but most had walked across the sun-parched earth to disappear into the hold. They had all come in pairs, silent except for the thrum of their feet against the earth as the steady procession continued.

They had begun to appear a week ago, a trickle to begin with, then a steady line of moving flesh, moving with a purpose towards the ship. At first, she and Silver had laughed at them from the safety of their hidden lookout.

"Come and see this," she said when the first pair stumbled from the mountain range below their lookout and headed out to the strange vessel. "When did that huge thing appear?"

Silver nudged her aside to get a better view and then snorted with derision. "Honestly, there is no accounting for the gullibility of some individuals. We got the same message, but do you see us following like sheep?"

Ruby gave a high-pitched snort of laughter as she sidled up to him. "They don't all have clever partners like you who know a scam when they hear one."

Silver preened and tossed back his mane of silver hair. Sometimes Ruby's silliness irked him, but when she made comments like that, he knew why he had chosen this dainty creature to be his mate.

"Enough of this. Let's go for a run and enjoy the heat of the day. We have better things to do than spend the morning watching those mindless creatures doing as they are told. We make our own decisions, and I say our time is better spent in the hunt."

"Of course, sweetheart," said Ruby, obeying him as usual. "Perhaps it will rain tomorrow, as the messenger promised, that's the one thing we can agree on. Mesopotamia has become as dry as a desert over the last few seasons. A light fall of rain would be most welcome."

"You are a funny little thing. Of course, it will rain soon. We did not need a messenger to tell us the weather. The rainbow that is even now lighting up the valley below us is all the proof we need."

"How strange that the rainbow ends exactly where the ship lies – do you think we may be wrong about the rest of the message?" From beneath her long lashes, she glanced at Silver as she spoke but knew his answer even before he replied. Male pride would never allow him to admit to her he had been mistaken.

"Of course I'm not wrong; you yourself agreed it is a scam. If we followed like the rest of those fools, who knows where we would end up." Without another word, he started to climb the mountain track. Sometimes her foolishness was not worth answering, let alone getting into an argument. He had given his opinion, and she had agreed with it, so why did she now doubt him? After this hunt, he would have to have a serious talk with her, reminding her who was the head of this relationship. Doubts crept in about his choice of a partner. If she could not agree with him in this, what future did they have together? The other males would laugh at him if they learned of her stubbornness to follow his lead.

The look on his face told her what he was thinking and, alarmed, she moved closer to him until they ran side by side. With a snort, he allowed her to catch up, pleased at her willingness to follow. When he caught sight of movement ahead, he drew apart and raced forward. By the time she reached him, he had brought down the prey – a fat bird with a large, heavy beak – too heavy to allow it to fly away. Watching him tear it apart, she glimpsed movement behind a nearby rock. Without a second's hesitation, she too pounced. This bird was identical to the one Silver had caught, only smaller. Obviously, the mate of the first one. She could not help but wonder if the two birds had been on their way to the ship. Well, now they would become a tasty meal instead, enough to last them for several days.

For the next hour, the pair ate in silence, both immersed in thought. Ruby could not shake her uneasiness about the messenger's words. No one else in the entire group had given it a second thought, though. Silver, oblivious to everything except filling his belly, carried on eating. So like a male, she thought, less fondly than she had before. The look in his eyes when she had questioned his previous judgment stayed with her. We can all make mistakes, she mused as she finished her own meal. However, he is so arrogant he assumes every word he speaks I must treat like a pearl of wisdom. I am beginning to think I may have chosen the wrong mate – when the rest of the group returns, I may well request a change of partner.

Silver caught the look of hostility in her eyes before she lowered her head to finish her meal. Without a word, he stood and began moving towards their campground. It lay some way ahead of their previous lookout point. Instinctively she rose and followed him, the silence between them deepening.

When they entered the ground, it was as empty as before, to the secret relief of both of them. Perhaps, Ruby thought, we need to talk this out. Maybe I am blowing this up out of all proportion. The sight of those couples disappearing inside that ship has unnerved me more than I realised.

Silver, too, was having second thoughts about Ruby's defiance. She was young – one of the youngest females in the group, and by far, in his opinion, the best looking. All they needed was to talk it out before it got out of hand. With that, he lay down next to her and apologised. She, recognising how much it had cost him to make the first move, nuzzled into him.

Next morning, curiosity drew them down to their original lookout. Today, according to the messenger, was the last day to board the ship. As they stood together and gazed at the huge wooden vessel, a loud rumbling filled the air. Slowly at first, unseen cables pulled the gaping entrance upwards. The opening finally closed, sealing the entire hull. When the creaking of pulleys stopped, Ruby and Silver waited to see what would happen next. Where could it go, this great wooden ship marooned on the arid plains?

They did not have long to wait – the morning sky darkened, and then a massive bolt of lightning pierced the blackness. Ruby gasped as the spiral horn on Silver's forehead blazed. She knew her own, too, glowed in the unreal light. As soon as the lightning bolt vanished, an enormous clap of thunder deafened them both. Then, the rains began.

This was not the gentle rain Ruby and Silver had discussed yesterday. This rain would become a deluge, the deluge a flood. The wooden ark with its precious cargo of two of every animal would float above the mountains to safety. Two of every animal - minus the horrified pair of unicorns that stood as if frozen amid the rising water. First, it covered Ruby's golden hooves. Before long, it soaked both hers and Silver's pure white flanks. When their flowing manes disappeared far beneath the water, the light of their magical horns dimmed forever.

Wendy Stackhouse

Ruby Rival

Voluminous folds of the gown swirled around her as the sequined hem brushed the floor. The slow spinning of the mirror ball above the opulent room highlighted the golden sheen of her dress. Tiny jewels shimmered beneath the many folds of satin material.

The mirror-ball, like everything else in this ornate ballroom, shone with weeks of attention. It reflected not only her dress but also the gleam on the golden floorboards themselves.

Heady with excitement, she was aware how the mirrors around the room picked out the precious gems scattered over her outfit. Arabella's breath quickened as she neared her goal.

At the end of the long room stood Prince Gustaff, heir to the throne and very much in need of a wife now his father lay dying of battle wounds. True, Gustaff had not inherited his father's good looks, or his gentle ways, if the rumours were true. However, Arabella convinced herself it was something a good wife could remedy. With the right courtly clothes and manners, even looks could change.

Since infancy, her parents encouraged her to believe she was destined to be a princess. Her beauty, they said, would make her rise above her station in life as the daughter of the King's Adviser. With her father's inside knowledge, she knew gold and jewels attracted the fickle young prince as much as a pretty face. Tonight she had all these attributes in abundance. Giving another twirl as she glided under the mirrors, she dared a look at the object of her desires.

Like every other male in the room, his eyes never left the

glittering figure that advanced so dreamily, it seemed, towards him. Tonight he knew he had to choose a bride – if his father died before he married, he could not take the throne. The law of the land stated his married cousin would inherit the throne if he remained single. He must marry, though remaining single was a state he much preferred. To continue carousing with his brothers-in-arms, visiting the village brothels, riding the best horses – his life was perfect. However, if he *had* to have a wife, this shiny creature heading towards him might do as well as any other. He knew when the great brass clock at the end of the room pealed twice – announcing it was 2.00am – he must pick his future bride. As soon as he held both her hands in his, it would signal he had made his choice.

A glance behind him showed the clock hands had but three minutes to go – it was 1.57am. Setting a smile on his face, he prepared himself to greet his would-be bride – then stopped.

Behind this shimmering beauty, a sensuous figure in a flame-coloured gown approached. No flounces of satin and taffeta swirled beneath the mirror balls. Instead, the raven-haired vision undulated – he could think of no other word to describe the way she moved towards him. The dress clung to every voluptuous inch of her figure, except where her magnificent breasts spilled over the top. Creamy white skin covered her back, a back that stretched naked to her waist. No jewels adorned her dress – she herself the only adornment it needed. A tiny groan escaped him. It echoed in the stunned silence of the room. Even the palace orchestra ceased to function.

Arabella, aware a hush had fallen over the room, glanced behind her to see the cause. Mouth widened in shock, she took in her Ruby Rival – a complete stranger. This girl had never appeared before in the palace or the surrounding village. The raven hair that fell like a waterfall of treacle around the girl's shoulders announced she was not of this country. No visiting dignitaries ever came with such a darkness of hair, or whiteness of skin, so where did she hail from?

Mind racing, Arabella recalled her father speaking of a country many moons travel to the north. This country lay covered in snow most of the year, and rumours spoke of the existence of a mysterious tribe. No traveller had ever ventured that far, so no one knew the truth of these tales. Between her country and this fabled one lay harsh mountains and lakes. Marauding tribes lay in wait for anyone who tried to cross the lands.

All this flashed through her mind as her ruby rival came closer, so close she felt the swish of those impossible midnight-coloured locks. Black eyes glittered as the girl drew near, and Arabella wanted to run from their malevolence. No words left either of their lips, but none seemed necessary. The race was on.

Three minutes left – only three – and it was unseemly to run. She managed another twirl, hoping to sweep ahead of her rival. Instead, the creature glided past her and leaned seductively towards the prince. His eyes followed every wanton curve, his head nodding in time to the sway of her hips. Tiny, delicate hands fluttered towards him. He stood only steps away from this exotic being.

Two minutes remained – only two – and Arabella was at a loss to think of something. She must attract the Prince's attention away from this interloper in deep red, and back to her own innocent golden sparkle. Other than stripping off her dress, she could think of nothing that would draw his eyes back to her.

In desperation, she did the only thing a well-brought up young lady could do.

With a determined twirl, she shoved her ruby rival aside with the sheer weight of her swirling, multilayered skirts. With half a minute to spare, she approached the prince and swooned at his feet.

The clock pealed twice as her body sank gracefully to the floor, and the startled young man took hold of her hands to break her fall. Cheers exploded throughout the ballroom: they had their new queen!

Wendy Stackhouse

This story came about from a unique writing prompt at the recent Shoalwater Retreat. We were each given a small cardboard paint sample from Australia's favourite hardware store. Each sample had on it the name of the paint colour, and a number. Mine was 'Ruby Rival 157'. Since then, I have been on the look-out for other unique prompts - a trip to the supermarket will never be the same again!

What's in a Name?

During the twenty years I was involved in Story-telling, I used that genre to find the history of my name, learning that I was named after a Goddess and debunking my mother's story that the name we shared was an old English one.

This discovery of the origin of my name, and the pleasure it gave me, was to become an introduction to a lesson that I presented when I was working in other countries. These were always two-way learning times as I learnt about the history of the names that the students had been given in countries where English was not their first language. The history of their family names showed where their ancestors had stood within their community, their clan, their religion and their tribe.

Babies are never just named: there is always a thinking about it, a compromise, a *knowing* when the mother holds her baby for the first time. The naming of the child can cause rifts in the family, threats of disinheritance and horror when new grandparents hear what they must call their first grandchild.

The classes I did storytelling with had their percentage of problem students. When I suggested they find out, before my next lesson, how they got their name, some were scathing that anybody would remember anything at all about them, let alone how they got their name thirteen or so years previously. These students were often the ones to come back with smiles on their faces as some very astute family member had recalled that the Mum, long gone, had admired a famous film star of her era.

Just as the learning of the history of my name enhanced my years of Story-telling across the other side of the world, so too did the name of one of my friends influence her life, her talents and her Art, and her movement across to this country: the other side of her world.

We met at the Eastern Goldfields Primary School, which is in Kalgoorlie. We had both been given an introduction by a mutual friend, which was to be like a golden key because we would not have paired off without that name in our hands. This new friend was not only a reclusive by nature but her art room was on the other side of the playground. It had originally housed THE SCHOOL OF THE AIR, which had sent, by radio waves, lessons to remote areas. This new friend only came into the staff room for the obligatory staff meetings.

Her childhood sights had been set on education as a way to escape the poverty and restraints of her home country, still trapped in civil unrest. With her education complete, she started the first step of her journey across the world and had settled under that hottest of suns on the red earth that were to have such an influence on her life. She taught me how to see art everywhere. We spent much time on our knees looking through the lens of her camera at plants sprouting in the desert after the first rains. She showed me how to take in the panoramic view, and she would pinpoint one thing, in that vastness, that enhanced the totality of the scene. She had found somebody that would walk out of the classroom, once a month, on a Friday afternoon, get into her station wagon and spend two whole days travelling across that desert, that red canvas, lit by the rays of the hottest of suns that was to influence her future and her approach to art.

Maybe the name she was given was the reason she resonated with the different light that the sun gave to that flat desert country we were moving around in, to the soil, to the air, and to the horizon-to-horizon panorama she filmed, then painted. The very first Laser Beams, which were invented to show details and depth and colour via a projected light, were generated by the gem Ruby: the name of my artistic friend.

Lavinia Tarrant

Time is the garden we prune

those ruby-red plums
decorate the window sill
the basket you bring home
full to the brim

we picked them all—
carried them into the house
rolled them on kitchen paper
doyleys wrapped their cheeks
folds   held their caramel in

Time is the garden we prune...
ruby ring on your finger
bought from a store in Hong Kong
—we walked the High Street
until we found the right one

time remembered
this time, this garden
pruned, as we turn the corner
recall ruby's red glow, sunset paint
sets her nails

ruby-time on her lips
velvet garden slips Revlon's
summer heat

we name her Ruby—
spray her face with small dots
a myriad flavours, ice-cream
musk, caramel, hazelnut, mint
she loves them all...

time is the garden we paint
as we sit in the alcove, blossom days
in an apple of nights   cherry pink
these are our dreams

winter's garden cultivates
the soil of our gaze

Rose van Son

Royal Ruby Affection

Royal lovelies
Undying love
Beauty everlasting
Yours forevermore
Romance captured
Underneath the gum trees
Bearer of the enchanting
Youthful glow vibrant red tones
Borne in the depths of the earth
Uniquely crafted by an unseen hand
Rough stones barely recognisable
Yearning to be revealed
Brilliantly cut, expressing timeless glamour
Upheld by tradition a gift for the rich
Resonance of being respected
Ultimately a show of affection
Belonging to a hopeful heart, an unadorned finger
Yielding the precious reuniting of two souls in love

Cheryl Workman-Davies

Search for Treasure

In the dim street light, something caught Henry's eye. He circled back. It was probably nothing. But he was drawn like a magpie to find the source of the sparkle.

Down the alleyway, his gumboots splashing in the muddy puddles of yesterday's rain, again he saw the glint of something special, and again he took the time to stoop down and check the abandoned treasure.

A discarded golden dollar, he sighed and pocketed the find.

The wind picking up caused him to shiver. He glanced at his cracked watch face to check the time and nodded. Perhaps it was ok to rest now.

He plunged his hand back into his coat pocket and reviewed the totality of his night on the hunt – three single dollar coins, a blue button, and a broken silver chain necklace. It was the kind that belonged on a pretty girl with a nice ruby pendant and earrings to match.

Henry retreated to his doorway a few blocks from his treasure field.

His body tensed as it so often did as he went to retrieve his meagre belongings. What if someone had taken them? What if he'd lost what little he had. But there they were. A small hessian bag with a book and a nobbly blanket sat on top of a few sheets of flattened old cardboard boxes.

Henry made his bed for the evening wishing the wind would go away.

Wrapped in his blanket and tugging down his beanie, he curled up on the concrete shielded by the layer of cardboard boxes, the only mattress he now had since becoming homeless.

Sleep never came easy, but as always, he was glad when it did, for it gave him a few blissful moments of escape from his failures as a man.

Heavy foot traffic, honking car horns, and roaring engines filled Henry's ears come the morning. Wafts of cappuccino, freshly baked goods, and rain met his nostrils.

Henry's stomach groaned, but it was way too early to listen to any of its cries.

The night's treasure hunt hadn't yielded nearly enough.

Eventually, though, Henry couldn't ignore the ache in his bones or the cramping of his muscles. The odours of the commuters reminded him of another time in his life. He stirred and stood and watched the passersby scatter. He didn't blame them.

Once he had rearranged himself, he looked to spot treasure abandoned by those more fortunate than he. Tossed food barely touched. He mentally made a list of desired food items and then played a game of find and seek.

Much like his nocturnal treasure hunts, Henry had a daytime hunting strategy too. He stalked the streets, checked the bins, and hovered like a seagull around cafés. An abandoned plate of food was to him a feast. A lifeline. A delicacy.

Grateful for every bite he managed to snag, the food gave his body fuel to get through the night. It gave him hope that if he kept on existing long enough, he'd find a way to recover his life.

After a full belly was accomplished, Henry curled up for a nap. He woke as the temperature took a dive as the sun disappeared from the sky.

Out on the evening hunt, Henry's task was simple enough: scour the streets and alleyways for anything useful. He'd got his precious blanket that way. Right now, he was saving his coins for a special visit to the salvos for a new winter jacket.

A glint of red flashed in the moonlight. The full moon providing ample illumination, Henry zoned in on the culprit; the small item beamed at him brilliantly. Henry sank to his knees and groped with his grubby fingers through the leaf debris. A loop of gold adorning a stone the colour of raspberries. A vibrant, bold red.

Henry sniffed the stone, the tiny crackle of hope lodging in his heart.

Could this be real?

He took a serviette from his pocket and carefully folded the ring inside.

He dared not believe until he knew, but he sat awake waiting for sunrise.

The shops began to open, and Henry waited by the jeweller, his life balancing on the precipice of change. The moment could mean everything would be ok. And with hope, he ventured into the store to figure out what he had found.

Cheryl Workman-Davies

About The Society of Women Writers WA

The Society of Women Writers was first established in Australia in Sydney in September 1925 to bring together women writers and journalists in New South Wales. Their aims were to be a social body; to promote knowledge of literature; to encourage women writers, and to strengthen the ties of interest between Australian and visiting writers (www.womenwritersnsw.org/history/).

Until the 1970s, the Society was based in Sydney, using a postal critiquing system to keep in touch. During this decade, branches were established in other Australian states and the first Federal Constitution was adopted in 1978 with an agreement that Federal responsibility be transferred from state to state every two years. Twenty years later, the decision was made to decentralise, each state forming its own Society.

The WA branch initially operated only through correspondence groups until the first President, Ethel Webb, was appointed in 1981, and members began to meet regularly. The Society of Women Writers WA was incorporated as an autonomous body on 25 February 2000.

Contact Details

The Society of Women Writers WA Inc
PO Box 434
Northbridge
Western Australia 6865
Tel: 0415 840 031
Email: swwofwa@gmail.com
Web: www.swwofwa.com.au

www.ingramcontent.com/pod-product-compliance
Lightning Source LLC
Chambersburg PA
CBHW030755190726
48285CB00003B/873